"The reader emerges from this unwavering view of life with the impression he has met and shared thoughts with a most remarkable old gentleman. . . . *The Heart of a Distant Forest* introduces an auspicious talent. . . . Williams' writing is colorful, knowledgeable, taut."

The Dallas Morning News

"*The Heart of a Distant Forest* grabbed my attention and my heart from page one and held both until the ending. . . . It has been a long, long time since I've felt as much genuine enthusiasm for an author's talent and sensitivity."

Eugenia Price

"A gentle first novel. . . . Lachlan rejoices so in life that it is impossible to pity him. His goals are modest: '1. Trim Mama's hedges back to their original shapes. 2. Go ahead and alphabetize my books. 3. Make up a calendar with birth dates of famous people and celebrate each one, maybe starting with writers. . . .' As Lachlan pursues these tasks, he records observations and moods in a delightfully straightforward manner. . . . we come to care and find ourselves moving eagerly with him from one day to the next."

The New York Times Book Review

THE
HEART
OF A
DISTANT
FOREST

Philip Lee Williams

BALLANTINE BOOKS • NEW YORK

"The Lifeguard" by James Dickey, Copyright © 1961, reprinted from
Drowning With Others by permission of Wesleyan University Press. This
poem first appeared in *The New Yorker.*

Library of Congress Catalog Card Number: 83-19384

ISBN 0-345-32365-3

This edition published by arrangement with W.W. Norton & Company,
Inc.

Manufactured in the United States of America

First Ballantine Books Edition: June 1985

*This book is for
Linda and Brandon.*

I wash the black mud from my hands.
On a light given off by the grave
I kneel in the quick of the moon
At the heart of a distant forest
And hold in my arms a child
Of water, water, water.
—JAMES DICKEY, "The Lifeguard"

THE HEART OF A
DISTANT FOREST

May 1

Morning is rising in silence. Nothing will happen along the green edge of the pond for several minutes more. I rest among a tangle of ferns. At the far edge of the water's edge are *Typha latifolia*, common cattails, erect and masculine, stalk-straight as the light edges from the east. I would like to crush their roots for flour. My pen makes noises like a frog, scratching, creaking. But there is no symbolism in this.

My grandfather made cane seats for chairs from cattail leaves, four of them around his table. He died long before I was born. That was 1906 when Samuel Lachlan passed on. When I came back from Europe in '45, the chairs were gone, replaced by captain's chairs from a mail-order house.

The light rises like the gentle upturning of a kerosene wick. Where are the night sounds? Why have they gone silent? Perhaps my frightful size cowers them into their own constricted shadows. There. The beaver is humping and going under out in the middle where it is deep and clear. Later, its broad tail will churn the liquid into whiteness.

I have come to my patronage now, alone and ready for what comes next. I have this time left, a year, perhaps less, they say. The stillness is in me, and I will try to listen well, to trace the trail of camphor weed in the thin woods and to merit the confidence of the blue heron and its snow-winged young.

I will sit here this morning until the bass begin to thrash. Then I will pass back up the hill with the morning noises, out of their fragile keeping, and fry bacon and make fresh biscuits.

My scent will follow me up to the house. Perhaps it will rain and be a good day for digging worms.

May 2

No rain. I have been thinking today of this house where an old man may ease into dreams once more. I won't repair it too seriously, for after me come the vines and the kudzu, twisting through the windows and over the porch. It is also their patronage.

My grandfather built it with his gnarled hands, one thick finger lost in a logging accident as a boy. Daddy used to talk about that missing finger, as if it still pointed sternly at him, regulating his chores and his timeless leisure along the banks of Shadow Pond.

It holds my books well, and my bed. Sunflowers have pushed against the eastern side now, bunched there as if huddling for protection against the shade of the water oaks and beeches. Some boards are lighter pine, replaced in the early '50s against a bitter winter when the pond turned to ice. But the old ones are firm enough. Charles is always impressed with its solidity. But he presses the point, aware of the brick expanse of his own home in town, perhaps a little guilty at his success.

The tin leaks only in a few places, and my crocks catch the water easily, comfortably. The red paint is something I remember, but it is all gone now and the rust is spreading from the chimney like a burnt-umber malignancy.

I sleep well in this house, especially when it rains. As it is not the season for showers yet, I sleep well anyway, and dream as I will of my classroom and the faces of farm boys long grown into age and children.

May 3

Charles came out to visit today, and we took the boat out in the pond about the middle of the morning. He is shaken that I refuse the treatments.

"It's nice to be able to come home," he said, aimlessly stirring the dark water.

"It's been kind of a dream of mine," I told him.

"Has it changed much?" His voice is still high and reedy, just as it was when we were kids together.

"What do you think?" I asked.

"I think it looks a lot like it did in 1918," he nodded. "I don't think it's changed all that much."

I lit my pipe and inhaled the sweet smoke, chewing on the stem.

"Maybe not. Maybe it hasn't changed at all. But I keep thinking there's something here I've missed. Maybe I'll find it."

"I guess we are the only things that have changed," he said mournfully. I nodded, with the worn briar hanging from the left side of my mouth. He asked me if I was feeling all right, and I said yes, I feel fine. It takes time to die, like anything else. He crossed his thin legs. It made him uncomfortable so I did not talk about it anymore.

This talk of dying is only God's gossip. I plan to live longer, much longer. We talked about his boy, Alex, who is now a successful banker in Chicago. He is just about the age my Jim would have been.

As we were paddling back to the shore, one of the beavers surfaced not far from us, his brown fur slick and oily, grinning before he plunged.

May 4

A good shower this morning. I spent the morning trying to find something appropriate to read. I found this haiku:

> *Spring rain;*
> *Rain-drops from the willow,*
> *Petals from the plum tree.*

I like that. The rain is intimate and dark. From my window, I could see the pond, and it turned a pebbled gray when the drops fell.

May 5

I have done something terribly wrong at some time in my life. No, not wrong. Evil. Some sin against God and man. But what is it? I never killed a man, not even in the war. That was for the privates, not the officers.

Did I commit adultery? No. That wasn't it. How could I have ever left Sara's side? Why do I feel this way today?

A cold front went through last night, and it was chilly today so I built a fire with old pine logs. It blazed too brightly and I splashed sand from the black iron kettle to keep it down.

The cedar tree by the corner of the house was wet all day, even with the wind, but the sky was a deep blue. In the cedar's wet limbs, a grackle eyed me suspiciously when I went outside in my heavy sweater for another log.

I was still bothered by the ghost of some past indiscretion, or even sin. Perhaps we need guilt as a buffer against too much pleasure.

I took a long nap in the afternoon. The scratching limbs of a nearby pine comforted me.

May 6

The Sullivan boy went fishing this morning at Shadow Pond, and I went down for a spell to keep him company. He had a pork-and-bean can full of calves' liver, and I was delighted with his dexterity in thrusting his thin hand into the can and coming out uncut with a dark red lump.

I had almost forgotten it was Tuesday.

"Why aren't you in school?" I asked gently. He pulled the glass rod over his shoulder and flicked the line out near a clump of lily pads.

"I'm sick," he said solemnly. He squatted on his haunches.

"Nothing serious, I hope."

"Sick of school," he shrugged.

"What you fishing for?"

"Cats. They're more liable to eat on the bottom. You just put some liver down there with a sinker, and they'll take it."

He cocked his head and stood slowly, quietly, his body rising like a flower stalk from the damp reeds. His right hand came sharply to his side and the line went taut as he reeled.

"Brother catfish," he exulted as he reeled. "Come in here you mudsucker." He wiped his left hand on his muddy jeans and continued to pump until the fish was at the shore, broken and worn from the fight. He pulled the line out and the catfish croaked as he slid it carefully on to the stringer.

"Don't let that son of a gun get you," I cautioned.

"I ain't. You know the best thing for a catfish cut?" he asked. He flung the line with the fish into the water's brackish edge.

"What?"

"Catfish. Smear catfish slime on the cut. It's the best thing. You ask anybody."

He rebaited the small hook, tying the liver firmly into place with fluorescent monofilament. He cast out to the same place as before and squatted. His head was bare, the hair cropped clean to the scalp. I heard the Sullivan boy got lice and had his head shaved. He handled the rod lightly with his finger on the line.

By the time I went back up to the house, he had four catfish. Later in the afternoon I walked back down to the pond, and he was lying there asleep in a patch of greening galax.

My mother planted it there years before when we had picnics by the pond. But now it has grown wild.

May 7

Spent today reading about the French Revolution. Teaching it always caused me problems. It wasn't that I admired feudalism that much, but perhaps that I feared anarchy more.

The anarchy of the peasants caused the National Assembly in August 1789 to start thinking of concessions. I have always believed in order. But at the cost of justice?

Now I resist the anarchy within my body chemistry. There should be some rational progress, but I know that changes will come with the terrible swiftness of the guillotine. I could never have been a Jacobin.

I believe in a pointless order, a wayward discipline. Both are better than anarchy.

And how I miss my pupils' eyes!

May 8

I went to town today and ran into Callie McKenzie at the power company where I was paying my light bill. We chatted amiably until I realized her eyes were full of pity for me. At least that's how it seemed.

It is a most unpardonable myth that women do not age gracefully. She is just as lovely as she was those years before. But our paths no longer twine. She believes in one thing, I in something else.

May 9

Depressed all day.

May 10

It is noon on a Saturday as I write this. Feeling much better today. Have plans to attend the Bethel Baptist Church tomorrow morning. I practiced singing hymns while I was shaving this morning.

My face still looks okay to me, haven't lost any weight. The hair still gray and thick, the sharp chin and broad nose. My eyes are clear, but seem more green than blue today. The mirror pleases me.

A flicker landed in the cedar tree where the grackle had been a few days ago. Its wild call cheered me, but when I tried to imitate it, it ducked its crimson head and flew off down toward the pond.

I got a nice letter today in my box from Louis Percy, a boy I advised at Mt. Russell and to whom I taught American Indian history one quarter. He will come by to see me next Friday, the sixteenth. I haven't seen him in six years, and he's now teaching history at the University of Georgia over in Athens.

Ate cornbread and sweet milk for breakfast, just like my mother used to make it.

This morning I started alphabetizing my books. Then I will catalog them on five-by-seven index cards. Too warm for a fire today.

May 11

Preacher Stoddard uses the New American Standard Bible, the only text besides the King James I can bear. He preached from Ecclesiastes:

> . . . man does not know his time: like a fish caught in a treacherous net, and birds trapped in a snare, so the sons of men are ensnared at an evil time when it suddenly falls on them.

I sang heartily: "Blessed Be the Name," "Only Believe," and "The Consecrated Cross I'd Bear." To my amazement, when Preacher Stoddard gave the call, the Sullivan boy, Willie, came stumbling down the aisle, his eyes wet and round.

May 12

I cannot describe how glorious today was. I got up at dawn and walked for miles through the woods with my notebook noting wildflowers: blue sage *(Salvia azurea)*, false dragon head *(Physotegia virginiana)*, and Queen Anne's lace *(Daucus carota)*.

The sun sprinkled rays through the towering pines, and I saw several kinds of lizards and even a gray fox.

I had the strangest feeling of all when it seemed all of them were waiting for me there in the deep woods. For a while, I pretended I was a Confederate soldier passing from the battlefields home to a worried wife and half-grown children.

They would be joyful when I came through the fields toward the house.

May 13

I am selfish and frustrated today, angry at being yet insecure, fearful. Eric Hoffer said the chief passion of the frustrated is to belong. But I cannot belong to nature, and I no longer belong to man, family all dead or dying or moved too far away to visit.

I tried chopping wood to soothe the anger, but it was warm and before long I will no longer need the splints of hardwood on my hearth. I quit that. When I shaved this morning, I saw ominous splotches on my face. What do they mean? I dwell on this too much. I will try to do better.

Tomorrow is the anniversary of the restoration of Charles II to the throne. I noted the occasion on my calendar and tried to read about it, but it seemed distant and cold.

I have begun to get terribly lonely at night and have been playing Strauss waltzes. But they remind me of Sara and our excursion to Europe in 1935, of linden trees and nightingales and heavy dark beer. We held our youth to us then like an overcoat.

"Do you ever think you'll always remember a moment?" she asked one rainy afternoon.

"I always remember things," I smiled gently. "I guess that's why I'm a historian."

"Dear, I don't mean history. I mean something about us that you will always remember."

"I will always remember your eyes."

"You seem so melancholy about it all."

"Just reflective, I suppose."

"Like the puddles reflecting the rain," she said thoughtfully, looking through the broad front window of the café.

She meant something but I never asked. The waiter came with another glass of dark beer, and we laughed and drank. Maybe the Strauss waltzes should remain in the record jacket.

I should go to town more and stop this silly self-pity. But all day I have been angry and upset.

Melancholy reflections seem to be an occupational hazard.

May 14

Walked up to Amos Crick's house near the church today, and he was telling me about the demise of the clan Renfro. We sat in his dingy parlor while his wife kept bringing us sweet tea. Amos is in his seventies, I guess, a good-for-nothing who's not worked for years. But he's an amiable sort and talks out of the side of his mouth like a gangster.

"Quarest thang, them Renfro boys," he drawled. "Old man named 'em Buck, Bob, Buley, and Ben. Just the lowest white trash you could imagine, you know. Well, seems this boy Buley, he's the one with the funny eye, found out he's got this disease that's gonna kill him soon, you know. So he takes this little money he's saved from pulpwooding over 'ar and tells his brothers he wants a good stone 'cause his paw's buried in a pauper's field. And he gives the money to Buck, who's the oldest, and them boys go out and drink it all up.

"Well, they comes back roaring drunk, and Buley's mad as hell at 'em. They tell him they done found a way that will not only mean they won't have to spend nothing on a funeral, but they'll actually make money.

"Buck says, 'We're gonna sell yore remains to the medical college over in Augusta. They pay right good. They're gonna study on you boy,' he says. Well, Buley goes into the other room all a-cryin' and a few minutes later comes back in with a thirty-ought-six rifle and blows 'em all to kingdom come. Ben lived long enough to tell the story, and then he kicks off, too. That's the end of them Renfro boys, I reckon."

He laughed and slapped his thigh and drew on his pipe. I was torn between wanting to laugh and get up and leave.

"That's awful," I said finally.

"Aw, Andrew, they weren't worth nothin'," he said out of the side of his mouth.

May 15

Wonderful news today. I have been invited to fly to Cheyenne, Wyoming, in August to lecture on Fort Phil Kearny. It's three months away, but I started getting all my books and photocopies together today.

I was pleased to find it still fascinates me. My biography I wrote on the commander, Henry Carrington, felt good in my hand as I went through it, underlining parts I will use in the speech. I made a tentative outline.

I wish I could have met Carrington, or Red Cloud, for that matter. Carrington would have made a fine dinner guest. What stories he could have told!

May 16

Willie Sullivan showed up at the pond very early this morning, and I walked down to talk to him. I expected his face to be full of his new faith, but I was suspicious since it is Thursday, and he should be in school. He was squatting motionless, watching the monofilament out in the dark water.

"Saw where you joined the church," I said. He stared straight ahead.

"Yeah, I did that," he said simply.

"Well, I guess you're happy about that."

" 's okay," he said.

"I mean you seemed really moved by it all. The whole church thought it was a fine thing."

He turned and stared at me with penetrating blue eyes.

"You was there?"

"Well, yes, Willie, I was there."

"My papa whipped my butt for doing that." I recoiled slightly, not knowing what to think.

"Why would he do something like that?" I asked.

"He said I made a fool of him." His voice was laconic and nasal, full of confusion about what had happened.

"How did you make a fool of him?"

"Didn't say. Raised a place on my rear end. He don't like me all that much, I reckon."

"There's got to be more to it than that." He slowly came up off the ground, staring at the end of the line in the water, but after remaining in a motionless crouch for a moment, he settled back down.

"If it is, I ain't found out about it."

Just then, the line jerked and began to spin off the reel as if he'd caught a shark. He let the line go out and then snapped the rod back over his shoulder. It took him nearly ten minutes to reel it in, a massive, sucking catfish with twitching barbels. Sweat was pouring off him as he dragged the flipping fish on to the bank.

I congratulated him on the fine catch and he seemed pleased.

May 18

Louis Percy came to visit Friday and we had a dandy time, but late in the day began drinking whiskey from my silver tumblers and as a result wrote nothing in the journal yesterday.

Louis had gained so much weight in the six years since I saw him that I scarcely recognized him, his face bloated but happy and his hands looking like hams. He brought with him his wife, Hilda, and their daughter. Hilda is also a vision of the distaff side of Jack Sprat, but the little girl, Marianne, is lithe and blonde and moved with an amazing amount of grace.

Among those who studied under me I always liked Louis best. He was absolutely dedicated to his topic, and never passed up a chance to ask my advice.

I told him about the invitation to Wyoming and he was pleased. We went into Branton and ate lunch at the Country Pine Restaurant, and I was amazed and a little shocked at the amount of fried foods Louis and Hilda put away. I made secret faces at little Marianne, and she kept giggling throughout the meal to her parents' consternation. We kept our secret.

It was cool and pleasant when we got back to the house, and we walked down to the pond and sat on the long bench my father made in 1922.

"It's good to see you feeling so well, Dr. Lachlan," Louis said, ducking his face. I laughed and patted him on the back.

"You've been hearing some horror stories about me lying down here dying, haven't you?" He flushed and looked uncomfortable. Hilda kept pushing her hair back from her pretty, fat face, while Marianne threaded through a thick stand of bamboo.

"They said you were sick."

"Well, don't pay your last respects yet, son," I said, feeling strong, believing then that I would have years more to live.

"You look like you'll live another seventy-five years," he said. For a moment, things were very uncomfortable. I knew he was trying to be affectionate, but such things have always embarrassed me. I just nodded.

They tried to leave about five, but I persuaded Louis to stay for one drink from the silver tumblers they gave me when I retired from Mt. Russell. The bourbon was good, and I silently thanked God there was nothing wrong with my stomach.

Alas, we drank too much and Hilda had to drive home, leaving me in a stupor in my house. I managed to strip my pants off and sank heavily on to my bed and slept through the evening and the rest of the night.

May 19

I am now sitting at the south end of Shadow Pond in some Johnson grass, watching *Castor canadensis* gliding through the still, thick water. His coat seems brighter today, a lighter brown. A few minutes ago, a retriever that belongs to Amos Crick suddenly came swimming through the water trying to catch *Castor*. But the dog was ludicrously mismatched in the water and merely yelped helplessly while the beaver flipped and slapped the water with his broad, flat tail.

Strangers seldom win the battle on an enemy's beloved homeland.

May 20

What use is there for sentimental old men?

Here are some things I plan to do to keep from being bored and useless:

1. Trim Mama's hedges back to their original shapes.
2. Go ahead and alphabetize my books.
3. Make up a calendar with birth dates of famous people and celebrate each one, maybe starting with writers.
4. Continue to be an Amateur Junior Naturalist.
5. Make an accurate map of Shadow Pond. Has anyone done this recently?
6. Go to town more.
7. Invite more people out for dinner.
8. Send off at least three articles to journals.

May 21

I went to town today and got a fine pair of hedge clippers at Mr. McAdam's hardware store. Got the kind with shock absorbers, and they look like they'll do the job for me.

Tom McAdam is about fifty, I guess, tall and lean. You can see the muscles in his cheeks when he talks. He laughs a lot and tells stories.

"What you going to do with those clippers, Mr. Andrew?" he asked me.

"Well, my mama planted hedges all over the yard some years ago and they've gone wild. Privet, boxwood, aucuba, gardenia, azaleas, viburnum. They've just turned into trees, sort of."

"I could get my boy Bill to come help you after school if you like," he said.

"Thanks, Tom, but I think I need the exercise."

"Well, it's getting warm so don't do too much."

"No, I won't," I laughed.

"Sure you don't want Bill to come out?"

"It would be all right with me, but he probably wouldn't want to."

"I'll tell him after he gets home from school today. He's a strapping buck. You'll like him."

May 22

Cataloging books all day. Pleasurable.

What is it about Willie Sullivan that intrigues me so? I fear it is the joy of seeing a child where I was a child, wishing it were all ahead of me again, that I could go gracefully through life without the burdens of age. But it is a joyful fear, one with anticipation but without expectation.

I began the day cataloging books, but I stopped for a while when I found an old copy of *The Last Days of Pompeii* by Edward Bulwer-Lytton. The pages are yellowed and slightly foxed, though the copy is less than seventy-five years old. I read the epigram from Cassius:

Day was turned into night, and light into darkness; an inexpressible quantity of dust and ashes poured out, deluging the land, sea, and air.

God, what that must have been like for those miserable people! Did they share that anticipation when the cloud descended, the terrible urgency of sudden chaos and the absence of order?

What really turned me pensive was the Song of Glaucus. Here is the part that troubles me:

Ah! sweeter to sink while the sky is serene,
  If time hath a change for thy heart!
If to live be to weep over what thou hast been,
  Let me die while I know what thou art!

May 23

I had lunch today with Charles at the Country Pine in Branton, and we talked about our school days in the teens in Branton, and we talked about our lives then. His vigor and enthusiasm surprised and heartened me.

"You remember Thelma Owens?" he asked.

"Yeah, yeah, Thelma. What happened to her?"

"She's still living in Atlanta, with her son now, I think. You remember the time she had that tuna sandwich in her desk and the ants crawled all over her?"

I tried to recall the incident, but I listened with pleasure.

"She danced all over the room," Charles said, laughing

out loud. "And Miss Bates asked her if she had ants in her pants and all of us back there knew what had happened and Petey Calhoun got to laughing so hard he wet his pants. Poor old Miss Bates got red in the face and didn't know what to do with Petey and finally told him to cross his legs until recess. The girls all smirked and giggled for the rest of the period, and poor Petey played hooky for three days until his old man beat hell out of him."

My friendship with Charles has never wavered, and he is the most even-tempered man I've ever known. I always regretted he never became a teacher, because he would have been a fine one.

May 24

It is night as I write this. I am in a clearing at the edge of the pond, listening to the crickets and the tree frogs. Light is never so rich as the darkness. Each man chooses the amount of sunlight in his life, drawing shades or opening them as his will dictates. Some must live in full sunlight and will fail without it. But many choose the shadows for their work and thoughts, the shuttered office or the shaded porch.

For now, at least, I choose this darkness, this small light from the kerosene lantern as my entrance into that other world.

What watches me as I rest here under this brilliant patch of stars? Am I more than another sound in the world of a cricket's daily scratchings?

I feel as if something has embraced me tonight and has held me with the endless wonder of maternal care.

May 25

Attended church today at the First Baptist Church in town and sat with Charles and his family. One of his grandsons and his wife are visiting and we all sat together in the back.

The sermon interested me not at all, and I spent most of the hour reading and re-reading Psalm 91: "You will not be afraid of the terror by night or of the arrow that flies by the day; of the pestilence that stalks in darkness, or of the destruction that lays waste at noon."

Somehow, this church seems less personal, more dedicated to answers than questions. Of course, there are no answers, but those things in which a person must believe should be as firmly fixed in his mind as the cycles of the moon.

May 26

Bill McAdam showed up this afternoon, a tall and muscular young man with fair skin and his father's light hair. He is pleasant and intelligent, and we talked some history as we sawed and cut at the wild hedges around the house.

"You know, I've never understood why the Indians just allowed themselves to be herded on to reservations, like the Cherokees walking all the way to Oklahoma. Why didn't they fight?"

"They did, as they could," I said, enjoying the feel of my new hedge clippers. "But it was really a matter of manpower and technology. When the smooth-bore muskets gave way to the repeating rifles, the Indians were doomed out West. There was one famous battle called the 'Hayfield Fight' near a fort in what's now Wyoming when the Indians charged, with far greater numbers, on a group of men cutting hay. The Indians didn't know the men had Spencer carbines and the fire was blistering. After that, it was clear to them that to fight was to die. That was the choice most had, moving or dying.''

"I would have gone down fighting," Bill said vigorously shaking his long hair. "They had to give up everything."

"It's hard to leave everything you love and never be able to return," I said. I looked around me at the land sloping down to the pond, at the weathered house. "That's something you never lose, though. The ones who lose are the children who sooner or later forget those sad stories and grow up as prisoners to some foreign ideology in a foreign land."

"It's like my daddy telling me about where he grew up in North Carolina," Bill said. "When he talks about the mountains, sometimes I think he's going to cry."

"It's easy to get attached to your home."

We worked most of the afternoon, and I felt refreshed with the work, our progress, and the talk with Bill. When he left, he shook hands with me firmly, a gesture I found somehow deeply touching.

May 27

I spent much of today reading a biography of Darwin. It is comforting to know the Christian missionary failed when he tried to convert the "savages" at Tierra del Fuego. Each man—or savage—should be allowed to believe, disbelieve, inhale, exhale, live, or die as he pleases.

A disturbing thing happened today. While reading, some passage reminded me of my father, but when I thought about him I could not remember how he looked. Somewhat in a panic, I sat for several minutes until his face suddenly appeared before me, not worn and shrunken as it had been before he died, but young and strong as it had been when I was a boy.

Darwin's naturalist work on the *Beagle* heartens me because I fancy myself somewhat of an amateur naturalist, though I have started far too late to know more than what amuses me. But had I started earlier, I would have been diverted so much by work that it likely would have made little difference.

I feel as happy discovering an Oconee Bell *(Shortia galacifolia)* as he did finding the skull of a Megatherium. But there are no Oconee Bells or Megatherium skulls here. I must be satisfied with less exotic pursuits.

The missionary on Tierra del Fuego failed because his logic was faulty. For the same reason, Darwin succeeded. I cannot tie any of this with the failure to remember my father's face.

May 28

Willie Sullivan dropped by after school today, soaked from the steady rain which has fallen all day. I was inside working on my books when I heard someone stomping on the porch as if buck dancing in slow motion. I looked through the front window and saw Willie knocking mud off his shoes, his thin face taut as he danced. His hair seemed to be growing out some, but it still stuck out all over his head.

I opened the door. The sky was laden and the rain was not hard but it fell straight down through the trees. Willie stood in front of me with his notebook in his hands, his face open, guileless, and his clothes wrinkled and dirty.

"Hello, Willie," I proffered. "Come in. You look like you've been walking in the rain for a long time."

"Just since the bus stop up on the highway," he said in his flat, nasal twang. "You got anything to eat, Mr. Lackland?"

"How about cornbread and milk?"

"Yessir. I'll take some of that."

I crumbled some cold cornbread into a bowl and covered it with sweet milk and handed it to him. He ate jerkily, like a dog too long lost and away from a meal. When he had finished, I did it again and he ate once more, this time more slowly, now starting to look up around my small kitchen.

"Willie, why haven't you been eating?" I asked.

"My old man's still mad at me and ain't letting me in the house, won't give me no lunch money for school," he said. We talked for a while, and I tried not to show how disconcerted I was that his father could have reacted so angrily to Willie's decision in church.

Evening came and I made us a supper of fried bologna and beans. By now, Willie had grown more pensive and went a long time between talking.

Finally, he asked if he could spend the night on my porch. I put my hands in my pockets and stared at him. He could not be much more than five feet tall, but he looked even smaller and childlike.

"Willie, I think you ought to be getting on home," I cautioned. "Your pa's probably worried about you. And your ma."

"Pa said I can't come until Saturday," Willie groaned, looking down.

"Where in the name of tarnation does he expect you to sleep?"

"He don't care. He still says I made him a fool."

"Okay, then, but you sleep on the couch, not on the porch."

"No, on the porch. It's all right. Just give me a quilt."

Now it is 10 P.M. and it is still raining and I can hear nothing but the rain gently tambourining on the tin roof. He has fallen asleep. I understand nothing at all of human nature.

May 29

Sara died five years ago today.

The years make us fear death much less. The season of white hair and infirmity is more joyous than I would have suspected thirty years ago. When I reflect on the deaths of historical figures, I see that in the end, they are no more or less than Amos Crick. That's what heartens people like Amos and reassures kings and emperors who feel trapped by the circumstance of power.

We are equalized by our obligation to die.

I thank Sara for sharing my life and for granting me now the multiple pleasures of solitude.

May 30

I forgot to write yesterday that Willie disappeared the morning after he came, before I got up. For some reason, I expected to find the blanket I gave him neatly folded, with a note of thanks pinned to it.

Instead, it was heaped near the fireplace where it had been walked on with muddy, sooty shoes and nearly ruined. I don't attribute this to any rudeness on Willie's part.

The rain has disappeared, so I went down to Shadow Pond about noon to gather cattails to cook, but the area was too swampy to reach. While I was at the edge of the pond, an immature great blue heron rushed overhead, its wingspan startling me. Just behind it came three ducks which splashed into the water near a clot of lily pads in the center of the pond.

Bill McAdam called and said he would come back over Saturday if I wanted him and I said, sure, come on over.

May 31

Bill and I spent a couple of hours this morning trimming back the rest of the privet, aucuba, gardenia, and such around the house, and while now it looks a little bleak, I know the shrubs will regenerate and become fuller.

Bill intrigues me. He is the perfect gentleman and always tries to say something interesting and timely. But he is also always trying to please me, something I find patronizing, if unintentionally so.

He has a keen interest in biology and is thinking about studying it in college though that is still a year and a half off. Not such a long time. Not nearly so long as he supposes at sixteen. After we ate sandwiches and drank cold milk, I took him out in the boat, hoping we would get a glimpse of *Castor* humping and splashing among the tangles of lilies and other aquatic growth.

A bass came leaping out of the water near the boat when we were idly drifting in the cool sunlight and startled us into exclamations. In the moment of a breath, it rose out, scales shining and then it disappeared into a quickly dissolving puddle of foam.

"I saw a big fish do that in the ocean one time when my Dad took me deep-sea fishing," Bill said, staring at the spot where the fish had gone under. "They do it sometimes to get rid of the remoras in their gills."

"So you're a fisherman, too?"

"I've caught two marlin," he said proudly. "Dad had them both mounted. You should come by and see them some time."

"Well, I'll do that, Bill," I said. "You do any fresh-water fishing?"

"We go trout fishing once in a while. I don't get too excited about the stuff around here."

After he left, I took a long nap in my bed and awakened feeling better than I have in days.

June 1

Memory is always a pleasant harbor. Going through some old papers in a trunk today, I came across a picture of me and my sister Anna taken when I was five and she was six. The picture was taken at the old park in Branton, long since turned into a parking lot for a grocery store. It was a pleasant green meadow with willow trees and one tremendous live oak. I recall sitting in its massive roots, pretending they were a throne and I a king.

I called Anna this morning in Hyannis where she lives with her son Paul, and his family. She was delighted to hear from me and a little solicitous about my health. But she was bubbling with fond news of her grandchildren.

I told her about the photo and asked if she remembered it.

"Andy, I sure do," she said. "Mama had this little box camera, and she used to sort of whistle when she wanted us to pose, and she took forever to snap the pictures. You just kept standing there and grinning no matter how long she took."

"Did we have Axel then?" I asked. Axel was our dog.

"Gosh, I just don't remember. Maybe. But he never came in to town. Papa wouldn't let him get into the car. You remember how Papa was about his cars."

After we hung up, I spent much of today working on my monograph about Branton's old courthouse, the one destroyed by fire after lightning hit it in 1922.

June 2

To my surprise, Callie McKenzie called today and invited me to have lunch with her at Nicholson's, a small, home-cooking place in town. Since her husband died several years ago, she has been getting more and more active in community life in Branton, having helped set up the first subscription concert series in the town's history.

While shaving I noticed that my face looked a little pale, despite having been in the sun much lately. I found this discouraging, but I feel well and shrugged it off.

I got dandied up after the shave with new cologne, feeling like a kid heading for a date. When I picked her up at her large, elegant house, she looked even more beautiful than I remembered, with her slightly graying hair and cool green eyes. She still has the most erect carriage of any woman I've ever seen, and I find it difficult to believe she is almost my age. I noticed that when I walked beside her, I stood a little taller than normal.

"Did you hear about that mess with the Renfro boys?" she asked as we finished a meal of black-eyed peas, collard greens, and fried chicken.

"Amos Crick was telling me about that," I nodded.

"Amos Crick? What were you doing talking to that old buzzard?"

"Oh, he just lives nearby."

"Well, I think it's the saddest thing. They had their whole lives in front of them."

"Not much of a life from what I hear."

"I suppose it's all in how you look at it. I mean, they were white trash and all, but to go like that." She shook her hair and clicked her teeth sadly.

"Things like that are always sad," I said. I couldn't take my eyes off her. We talked for a while about the town, about politics.

"Reagan scares me," she shuddered.

"That doesn't sound like the voice of one of Branton's conservative old McKenzies," I teased her.

"Well, before I was a conservative old McKenzie, I was a fiery young Kelley," she laughed. "Don't you remember Papa? He was in the legislature and spoke out for women getting the vote and was treated like a traitor to his country the next time he came back to Branton."

I nodded, warmly remembering old Sam Kelley, a man whose one term in the state house threw the entire district into turmoil. A local man challenged him to a duel one time.

"And Papa went to his house and just beat the hell out of him in front of his wife," Callie laughed. "That was the last time that man ever voted, they said."

We went back to Callie's house. Her maid, a gentle young black woman named Laura, served us hot coffee on a silver coaster.

When I got home this afternoon, I wondered what it was I felt for Callie—friendship, affection, even love.

June 3

I went for a long walk in the woods today to look for wild-flowers and was startled to find Willie Sullivan sitting by a small fire on the banks of Marble Creek.

"Willie, what are you doing there?" I asked. I startled him and he jumped up in a crouch, ready to fight.

"Mr. Lackland, you like to scairt me half to death," he said.

"I'm sorry, Willie. I just wondered what you were doing there with that fire."

"Watchin' it burn up," he said, as if I had asked a silly question.

"I mean, why did you build it?"

"To watch it burn up." He looked at me as if I were trying to ferret out some answer he didn't have.

"You mean you just like to watch fires burn?"

"Don't rightly know," he said. "I just felt like watchin' something burn up. Don't you never feel like watchin' nothin' burn up?"

"I guess so," I admitted. "I mean it's getting hot these days, and it's not the time you'd want to build a fire."

"I wasn't building it for the heat." He settled back down on his haunches and stared into the flames. "And I don't need no light." He took a slim pine stick and stirred the ashes.

"Well, just be careful with it and don't let it get away from you."

"I know how to keep a fire down."

All I found were some more false dragonheads.

June 4

A man's religion is nobody else's damn business.

June 5

The days have shaded forward from warm to hot now, and the long days of an idle summer are upon me. I have always fared well in summer, from those days when my feet were all callous until now when a stone bruise is unacceptable.

As a teacher, summer for those fifty years always meant a period of enforced absence from the Battle of Hastings or from Colonel Chivington's massacre of the Cheyennes at Sand Creek. Sara and I would often travel across the country, camping at sites we wished to explore—the terrain, the faces, the smell of the earth or plants we could not grow at home.

But summer, too, has its history, its internecine struggles, and its seasonal dynasties rising and falling in their natural order. The coming warmth reminds me that there are no regrets or fears in nature, only the acceptance of the possible and immersion in life too fertile for fantasy.

June 6

Listened to Beethoven all day while I worked on the books. I am surprised to find I have more fiction that I recalled, though I cannot remember how many of them were first Sara's.

I found two old books I know are mine, ragged copies of *Le Rouge et le Noir* and *Les Misérables,* the latter I first read as a kid and the former in my twenties.

I pondered for a time on Jean Valjean and wondered if my suspicions that I had done something evil those years might not have something to do with his dilemma of being discovered to have been an escaped convict. Do we all fear something we have done will undo our present good deeds? Or do we fervently wish that we can escape into irresponsibility from the burden of morality? I have no idea.

June 7

I dreamed last night I was in bed with C.M. and that we were having sex. The dream was incredibly real.

I was happy, excited, and a little ashamed when I awoke. Perhaps I should seek some feminine pleasure again.

I believe I shall.

June 8

It is night now and wonderfully cool. Today, I invited Harold Simpson out to go fishing in Shadow Pond and he arrived about six. Harold is now vice-president of the Branton National Bank and is as broad as he is tall. He is what once might have been called "jolly," though that word is out of fashion these days.

He told amusing stories while we drifted in the boat.

"Had a man come in a few weeks ago who wanted to put his wife up as collateral for a loan," he said as he cast out into the water.

"Not really."

"Damndest thing. I asked him what he wanted the loan for, and he said for farm supplies. I asked him what kind and he said for fence posts, barbed wire, some sheet metal, and copper tubing."

"*Copper tubing?*"

"I think he let that slip," Harold laughed. "Of course, he was going to build himself a new still, and we weren't about to get mixed up in that."

"Not even for his wife."

"He said she could be a maid for me if he missed a payment. Then he winked and said she had the hottest oven in the country. I asked him if she ever burned up the biscuits. He grinned and said, 'Ever oncet in a while.' He was real glum when I told him I was sorry."

I surprised myself by asking what his name was.

"Well, I suppose it don't make much difference, but I really shouldn't tell."

"I understand."

"Oh, hell, you know him. It was old Amos Crick up the road there."

"You're kidding."

"God's my witness. I think he would have let his old lady come over."

I tried to think of what Dorothy Crick looks like. Seems like she's a lot younger than Amos, maybe only in her early fifties or so. Kind of short and round and open-faced.

I caught three bream and Harold caught two bream and a small bass and he gave them to me. I cleaned them on the front porch and fried them for supper and ate them with buttered bread and some homemade applesauce I got at a store in town.

June 9

Watched television during the day and slept quite a bit. The fishing trip yesterday pretty much did me in.

June 10

I sat in the rocking chair on the front porch today and read my Bible awhile and watched birds.

Nothing unusual in the way of birds. Brown thrashers, blue jays, and a few robins. It hasn't rained for several days now, and they seemed to be having trouble locating food, even under the trees where the earth stays damp.

One interesting blue jay stayed much closer to me than the others. It had a withered claw and hopped about quite well on one foot. Yet the other birds seemed to shun it as if it were somehow guilty of having strayed too close to some predator. But it may have been a defect of nature. I kept expecting to see the bird totter and fall over, but it remained perfectly well balanced and when it burst into flight, it seemed no different from the others and flew with them as an equal.

I remember seeing an old blind dog one time that lived outside a friend's house at Mt. Russell. Though the dog could see nothing, it never stopped running around and knew where every stump and blade of grass was within two hundred yards of the house. Sometimes, it would sit very still with its nose in the air, trying to scent what it could no longer chase.

I wish I could be that adaptable and could treat my illness as merely another withered claw or failing eyes. And so today I praise the strength that still courses through my hands and the joy of seeing the sunlight scattered on the pine needles.

June 11

Night. Stars. Why did man believe that the sun circled the earth? Early scientists postulated eighty epicycles to account for the movement of the planets around the earth. I am awed by the leap of reason that led Copernicus to claim that the planets circled the sun. Yet even he could not completely discard the epicycles because he believed that the perfect heavenly bodies must move in circles, not in elliptical orbits.

This belief that the heavens were perfect and incorruptible was an important part of medieval thinking.

History has taught me to believe in the incorruptibility of nothing, least of all the heavens.

Therefore I mourn the loss of my innocence just as these medieval folk mourned the loss of the earth as the turning point of an ordered universe.

June 12

School is out now and Bill McAdam dropped by this afternoon. Young Bill and I have struck quite a friendship. To my astonishment, he began telling me about his newly failed love affair with a girl named Gretchen.

"It just didn't work out?" I gently probed.

"You never really know," he said. "You want something so much it hurts to think about it. It hurts me to think about her, but there's nothing to be done about it. She gave me back my friendship ring and everything. Lord, I miss her.''

''Did she say why she didn't want to go with you anymore, Bill?''

''She said she still wanted us to be friends,'' he snorted.

''The kiss of death,'' I said, shaking my head.

''But she's so pretty,'' he said softly.

I told him the same thing happened to me years before, but I didn't tell him the girl was Callie McKenzie.

June 13

Savannah. On the spur of the moment, I packed a bag and drove the 250 miles to the beach here, taking lodging at a wonderful old motel on the beach.

The sand on the beach keeps being moved away by shifting winds and tides, and though they pumped the beach back up a few years ago, it is now receding. The ride down was tiring, but I seem to have weathered it well. It was pleasant to be able to pick up and leave when the desire strikes.

For some reason, I can't seem to stop thinking about Willie Sullivan. I saw a boy squatting in the sand at sunset today and he looked like Willie, at least his silhouette did. But when he stood, he moved with the studied gait of any boy and not the simple graceful stride of Willie.

It is deep night now, and I feel lonely and sorry for myself. Tomorrow, I will find someone to talk to.

June 14

I must be more forceful. I must not look back. I must do something I have never done before. In the six weeks I've been keeping this journal, I haven't learned a damn thing.

Later. I wrote the above this morning, but it is now late afternoon and I have been drinking. I still agree, which must mean something.

Or else it doesn't mean a damn thing.

There is a woman sitting on my bed. She is fussing at me. I can't remember her name.

June 15

Her name is Janet. She is still here.

June 16

I feel lazy and indolent and I laid on the beach today until I was burned raw. I'll pay for that.

I have a cut on my back. From a fingernail, I believe.

I am joyously afflicted with my flesh.

June 17

The bitch rolled me.

I have been thinking all morning about the rare medicinal qualities of penicillin.

I haven't felt this cocky in fifty years.

Thank God for American Express.

June 19

Terribly ill for two days, not well enough to drive home. The price of pleasure shall be exacted. I am a tired old man.

June 20

Made it back home today, feeling stronger and exhilarated at my little escapade in Savannah. That's not like me at all. A good sign.

I watched a pair of cardinals for a long time just as darkness fell. They sat in the limbs of my apple tree in the front yard, as if expecting the blossoms to turn into fruit at any moment. That's the dilemma: sweetness is a long time coming and never as blessed as the wait.

I am sitting in my bed now, and I prayed for a long time because it is a help. I'm not sure what I prayed about because I kept having to thrust Janet from my intercessions with the Almighty. I'm sure He understands and will look upon me with charity when I stand before Him.

June 21

I asked Mr. Sullivan if I might take Willie to Athens with me this morning, and he shrugged his shoulders and said, "yeah," so Willie got in with me and we drove off. We went to the library at the university where I did some research on my upcoming paper I will give in Colorado.

I was touched by his solemnity as he sat in a straight-back chair and looked through a picture book of the Old West. On the way home, he talked about it.

"I could shoot an Indian," he said with his nasal twang.

"Why would you want to do that?"

"They was always killing the white folks."

"Maybe the white folks started the killing, Willie."

He thought a moment.

"Naw, the Indians done started the whole thing."

"How do you know?"

"I seen it in a movie on TV."

"But I thought you were a Christian now, Willie. Surely as a Christian you don't believe in killing."

"I believe in killing some people. I sure do that."

I didn't ask him what he meant.

June 22

The earth obeys its cycles. I was astonished to learn that to-day is the anniversary of Galileo recanting his brilliant thesis, and I wondered what a misfortune for humanity that was.

Science has always been the cross of theology. We were bemused but not surprised at Leakey's discoveries at Oldu-vai that man is millions of years old. And scant centuries before, Bishop Ussher pontificated that the earth was created in 4004 B.C.

One order is replaced by another and each has its season. I see reason in such order, but there is a time to admit that the method with which you have ordered your universe has failed the frontiers of thought and the microscope.

Today is the first full day of summer. A Sunday, I noted.

June 23

It is Midsummer Night by lantern light in my boat on Shadow Pond. None of the creatures of the water defend their territory against me. But I am not their lord. Once I was merely the egg, no more than the roe the female cat-fish carries in her belly deep in the mud. I was female, ovarian, descending until the sperm broke through and encysted.

And so was Napolean and so was Darwin and so was Amos Crick. There is nothing profound in this, but here under the stars I take a small counsel for the comfort of it.

A turtle bubbled up near me a few moments ago and then flipped down again. I did not see it resurface, for it does so with grace and cunning. It is said the giant tortoise of the Galápagos lives more than two hundred years. Perhaps one is still living who was bellowing his first air when Washington knelt at Valley Forge.

The turtle's ignorance of history is surely a kindness we may be permitted to envy.

June 24

Bill McAdam drove out today. He seemed calmer and full of brightness.

"Gretchen and I finally got back together," he said shyly.

"Well, that's good news, Bill," I said as I lit my pipe.

"We had a long talk. She said I was getting too serious and it scared her. I told her I didn't mean to crowd her, you know, and we talked it out and she took the friendship ring back."

"She doesn't just want to be friends anymore?"

"Not from the way she acted." He rubbed his face and grinned, and I grinned, too.

"I hope it works out all right."

June 25

Order is what I'm looking for. I sense it is around me, hidden somewhere among my ruins like an undiscovered Roman coin, still bright after having weathered all wars. Why do I fear the anarchy within me?

June 26

It is a pleasant Thursday, and Willie and I are sitting on the bank fishing as I write this. The fragrance of honeysuckle is bright upon us.

WILLIE: You ever got lice, Mr. Lackland?

ANDREW: No, I never did. You got them? *(I look at him suspiciously.)*

WILLIE: They get on me come summer. I hate them things.

ANDREW: If you keep your hair clean, you won't have them. Don't they have a medicine for that?

WILLIE: That stuff stinks.

ANDREW: Is it worse than having lice?

WILLIE: *(Brightly.)* Shit, yeah. I mean, I don't like to keep itchin' 'em and all, but that stuff makes you smell like a mule in heat.

ANDREW: I don't think mules get in heat.

WILLIE: Then like chicken turd. You rather have lice or smell like chicken turd?

ANDREW: That's not a very good choice either way, is it.

WILLIE: *(Scratching.)* No sir, it ain't a good choice at all.

ANDREW: Maybe you just ought to use shampoo.

WILLIE: Be okay by me, but my old man says he'd as lief have a cheap whore in the house as that perfumey stuff. He don't allow nothing with scents like that in the house.

ANDREW: Doesn't your mother use perfume?

WILLIE: You kidding? My old man'd beat the hell out of her if she wore any. He says there ain't nothing worse than cheap women.

ANDREW: *(Thinking of Janet.)* I understand.

June 27

Been reading Frederick Hulsey's book *The Human Species*. He writes:

> A scientific explanation, like a philosophic one, must be rational and logical, but it must be more than that. It must account for evidence as well as logic.

Having no grasp on logic and lacking evidence of the most rudimentary sort, I must hope that I remain rational for the remainder of this late season.

I suspect that, on the whole, this is a good life. For this assertion, I lack the patience of logic and ignore the evidence of petty jealousies, famine, and conflagration. And yet, somehow in the pulse of these woods, I feel there is something decent and good that binds us through the terror of the dawn.

When dawn comes, we can calculate our losses. But oh, the night!

June 28

My idol when I was a kid was Professor Thomas Andrews. They called him "professor" here in Branton, though he didn't even have a college degree. He taught history and biology at the Branton Male Academy. After public schools came, he never did make the transition and became a recluse at his house on the corner of Elm and Young in town. Sometimes Daddy would drop by to visit him and I would have to sit in his overstuffed sofa while he and my Daddy talked.

I remember him violently arguing against Teddy Roosevelt one time. He was an immensely tall man with a white beard and a pince-nez that kept falling into his lap. His wife would shuttle in quietly with coffee and then escape gratefully back into her sitting room. The parlor was full of heavy furniture and thick red velvet curtains that always reminded me of "The Raven" by Poe.

I can't remember why he hated Teddy Roosevelt.

One time, he got a flask from a burled walnut secretary that sat ponderously in one corner of the room. He tried not to let me see it, but I knew what was going on. Mrs. Andrews came in about that time and flew into a rage. I remember what she said:

"God have mercy on you, drinking that stuff in front of a child!"

I looked away and tried to pretend I wasn't in the room. I remember I felt ashamed for my father, knowing how he must have felt. But Professor Andrews looked at her with such a terrifying glare that she bowed almost like a geisha and slipped out of the room.

On the way home, Daddy asked me if I knew what they were drinking and I said yes and he asked me not to tell Mama, and I never did.

It was the first time I ever remember feeling that strange mixture of power and shame. As a teacher, I learned more about it than I wished to, but it taught me that a cheerful lie is no more harmful than a spring rain.

June 29

A very melancholy day here in this hot house with the tin roof.

I read some Shakespeare sonnets, but fell into a brooding silence when I came across Sonnet 22 and its ending:

Presume not on thy heart when mine is slain:
Thou gav'st me thine not to give it back again.

And so on this Sunday, my heart is neither mine nor God's, but Sara's, there with her where rest is the pulse of the earth.

June 30

Yahoo! I am drunk with the pleasant heat on my face as I plow up a spot in the side yard for beans. I will plant Jackson Wonder bush beans, butter peas, pole beans, and perhaps some okra. I rented a tiller from the hardware store and brought it out this morning in the trunk of my car. The thing beats the hell out of you!

What a wonderful feeling to ache from hard work. I feel the blood opening up old veins I thought long since collapsed and my head seems clearer than in weeks. I have the sacks of beans lined up here on the porch, and I have a ten-pound sack of fertilizer.

Perhaps I will plant nine beans rows like Yeats at the Lake Isle of Innisfree. I will watch them grow in ordered spaces. I will keep them safe from drought and insects. I will plant marigolds all around to drive off the insects.

I think I'll have some lemonade before I start back.

Tomorrow a new month and a new beginning for things that drink from the earth.

July 1

Planted, watered, fertilized.

Charles came by after lunch and we sat on the front porch for a spell and talked politics and so forth. About the middle of the afternoon, the sky turned charcoal and a dash of lightning was followed by a tremendous downpour that sent us scurrying around the house with pans to catch the water that came through.

"Why don't you get this roof fixed?" Charles asked.

"For what?" I laughed. But it didn't seem funny to him, and on reflection, I found it a rather stupid comment that I knew he took the wrong way. Rather than compound my stupidity, I let the remark pass.

When the colored butter beans come in, I will get some cornbread and streak-olean and cold buttermilk and sit on the porch just before the sun goes down and eat it.

July 2

Could it have turned out differently? Could I have been a banker or a mayor or the one with power now? Could Sara have been a senator now that women are taken seriously in politics?

I think of something I read in Gibbon: "In every age and country, the wiser, or at least the stronger, of the two sexes, has usurped the powers of the state, and confined the other to the cares and pleasures of domestic life."

I have confined myself to these domestic pleasures now. But no one is left with the power I could have once shared.

July 3

Today is Franz Kafka's birthday, but I will not celebrate it.

July 4

Late. Went into town for the parade and fireworks. Had a great time. Took Callie to the park and we ate barbecue and stew together, and I showed her the right way to sop up the stew with her white bread. We walked back up the sidewalks under the water oaks to the civic center where the fire department shot off some nice fireworks. One went askew and landed in the yard of Cleotis Spencer, a really dour old man who, we heard, was calling down all sorts of imprecations on the holiday as he beat out the flames in his grass.

The Air Force band played and we watched the bombs in the air, and Callie and I stood close, so close I could smell her perfume, which was vaguely flowery. Everything was rather ruined when the police arrived and pinched a young man for trying to lift a tape deck from a car in the parking lot, but everyone tried to pretend that such things were only incidental to what we were celebrating.

July 5

Something terrible has happened.

July 6

I couldn't write about this yesterday. They found Willie Sullivan's father dead, apparently from a heart attack. His heart stopped as he sat on a soft couch. Willie is missing, and the police and his family are worried about him. I feel ashamed for him, as if my shame could atone for his disappearance at such a time.

I walked up to the Sullivan place this morning, and there were old, beat-up cars all around it, and the strong smell of turnip greens and fried chicken. Several people were sitting on the porch, rocking and smoking, and inside, Mrs. Sullivan was lying on a couch, occasionally jerking as if being shocked, moaning horribly, being fanned by a tremendously fat woman I took to be her sister. I merely nodded my condolences and left a nosegay of wildflowers I picked along the lip of Shadow Pond.

"It's a tragedy," I said to a tall, thick man rocking on the porch.

"I knowed he'd come to an early grave," the man nodded. His teeth were crooked, stained like old piano keys.

"Are you a relative?" I asked.

"Cousin," he nodded again. I had the oddest feeling his head was only slightly attached to his neck and might, at any moment, fall off.

"I'm truly sorry," I muttered.

"I appreciate your regrets," he said.

"I guess y'all are worried about where Willie is."

"Yeah, but we know why he's gone. Hated his old man something terrible. People go crazy like that sometimes. That boy's always been odd. A real odd one."

"Oh, maybe not that odd," I countered, bewildered. "Willie's not that bad of a boy . . ." I stopped, something constricting in my throat. "I see him at the church and in town sometimes." My heart was racing as I lied.

I walked home through the woods, wondering if I might chance upon Willie squatting near a rotted pine log, unaware that his father was dead, or knowing, having watched him collapse.

I worked in the garden this afternoon, but I was troubled, and kept stepping on the rows where I had planted.

July 7

Bill McAdam has a new girlfriend and when he came out today he did not mention Gretchen. How easy it must be to transfer your affections with world enough and time. My affections linger far after there's need for them, for I cannot bear the idea that no one will be there to receive them later and that I will be left alone with a pointless concern.

I asked Bill had he heard about the Sullivan man and he said yes, but he didn't know much about it. He said no serious search had been made for Willie because he chronically ran away from home, and his mother was furious at him.

"So they haven't heard from Willie yet?"

"No sir, not as I've heard of. Course I don't know him, never laid eyes on him. They're going to bury the old man tomorrow and they think maybe he'll show up for that."

"Maybe he will," I sighed.

We talked about Indians, and I told him about General Connor's Powder River Expedition of 1865 and how one column had to shoot their horses, 900 of them, when they got bogged down in the snow. He seemed greatly impressed and asked me more questions than I had answers for.

He is so full of curiosity and eager talk. His eyes are bright and it makes me feel good to tell him what I know. Why does he care about what I know?

Why do I feel incapable of truly caring for him?

July 8

"A generation comes and a generation goes, but the earth remains forever."

The pastor read Ecclesiastes over the grave of Mr. Sullivan in the family cemetery down the dirt road about a mile from here. It was terribly hot today, and even under the tent,

I could see sweat streaming off his widow and the two men who were supporting her.

There was no church service. The coffin was covered with pine boughs, and once, a blue jay landed in the limbs and lingered there until the wide hand of the funeral director waved it away. I could hear a car scraping down the road occasionally, but mostly the only sound I heard was the hushed sobs and the flat words of the disinterested minister.

Yet I felt humbled by death as we all do, facing it there, fearful that one day we will come to the same end, stiff, hands folded, eyelids closed unnaturally, too thin, a little tight at the edges. I will come to that, no matter what good works I do now. And so it was even with Mr. Sullivan, a man I had every reason to dislike. I felt sorry for myself through him because he mirrored what I must soon become.

Now he was no different from any man's father or son who had gone to rest among the quiet shadows of the dead.

July 9

Being Respighi's birthday today, I listened to the *Pines of Rome* but got little pleasure from it. I keep thinking about death like a child thinks of Christmas coming.

The weather remains hot and dry. I began working today on a monograph about Ridgeway Glover, a photographer for Frank Leslie's *Illustrated Weekly,* killed at Fort Phil Kearny in 1866.

July 10

What's the use in keeping a journal?

A good question, but it relates to keeping the order written down, I think, rather like noting your blood pressure every day, not because you really give a damn, but because it convinces you that you still have one.

I don't think I can keep writing every day. I haven't felt too well. The heat is bothering me and there is nothing I can do about it. I am having pain in the area of my kidneys. Perhaps it has spread there. I don't have any energy.

July 11

I cried today for no reason.

July 12

Feeling better, stronger. Pain missing this morning in the kidneys. Perhaps something temporary after all.

My books are a great comfort to me. I do not remember where some of them came from. Today, I found three books that interested me greatly: *Catherine of Aragon* by Garrett Mattingly, *White Fang* by Jack London and *Rasputin the Holy Devil* by Rene Fulop-Miller.

Does it admit to weakness to admire physically strong men and women? Not that I admire an insane monk, but I am in awe of anyone who survived what he did.

I lingered awhile between the pages of these books and reflected on some of their sentences as I ate a ham and onion sandwich. The Vidalia onions are starting to come in.

July 14

He is here. Sitting there near the window, fingers drawn into claws, his face dark and unseasonal. He appeared while I was sitting near the pond watching *Castor* in his morning ablutions, humping spray across his darkness as he churned.

I was sitting there with my knees drawn up to my chest, mumbling over my mortality when I saw him standing near a beech tree, his hands limp beside him as if he were about to dash off.

"Willie," I said quietly, not a question or an explanation, a soft word for one in pain. He said nothing. He walked slowly toward me, his eyes had sunken in his face and his bones made impossible angles through his clothes as if he were starving. He stood by me but looked away, out across Shadow Pond. I spoke to him, but he did not answer or look at me. But he kept inching toward me like a weak magnet drawn to another's weak pole. His hands opened and closed convulsively. I watched his hands. I sat back down. He kept standing and looking over the pond, cavernous, sunken, terrified.

"I'm sorry about your papa," I said finally. He looked

down at me accusingly, as if I had broken some code that forbade the mention of his father. His head went down a bit, almost as if beginning to acknowledge my condolences, then stopping for fear of becoming too vulnerable for comfort.

I talked to him for a while, trying to help him.

"I remember when my pa passed on," I said. "It was fall, a beautiful day, crisp, clear. He had been sick a long time and his room smelled of camphor and roses. My mother put fresh roses there, the wild ones, until they all shriveled up on the vines that summer. We all agreed it was a terrible thing, to die, but Pa, well, he stayed propped up on the pillow and his eyes were alive, curious, hopeful.

"Well, I know this doesn't mean anything, but maybe death is something that's not so bad. I don't know. We've all got to do it. That's all I know. If a man could tell, he'd have more power than any man who ever lived."

I felt a little sanctimonious, but he seemed to be listening. It is late now, and after he ate supper with me, he fell into a chair and his eyes slowly closed. I covered him with a light blanket. His face is dark and so are his eyes.

I have never, never in my life suffered.

July 15

He was gone when I awoke just at dawn today. He took my bread and a large jar of peanut butter and my gallon jug of cold milk.

Should I call his mother or the sheriff? There is no proper order for this. It does not fit into what I have planned for these days, but somehow, I feel as if some power there in the trees has pulled me here for this and other things, perhaps greater things to come.

July 16

Poor Ridgeway Glover. Cocksure, brimming with desire to photograph the West. September 16, 1866. He decides to walk back to Fort Phil Kearny from a woodcutting party. They find him the next morning full of arrows.

What is it like to feel a dozen arrows suddenly becoming part of your body? Fools always die slowly, it seems. Or else they die quickly. It doesn't matter.

Here is what I did today: watered the garden, worked on the monograph, catalogued sixty books, and listened to a baseball game on the radio (boring).

July 17

I surprised myself by stopping at the country dog pound on the way to town and looking over the dogs there while talking with Jack Golden, the supervisor. I got myself a puppy.

He is all black, maybe part Labrador, fractious and full of humor. I've spent part of the afternoon trying to think of a good name for him. I've never been good at naming animals. I had a dog once named Jake, but I can do better.

I'm going to call him Africa. It has a nice ring to it, I think. He sleeps with his head between his paws and snores. Right now, he is sleeping and twitching and running at the same time.

It's hard to sleep when you are young because so much awaits you, and it is hard to sleep when you are old because there is so little.

July 19

Africa tore up part of my garden and I was very angry at him and chained him to the porch. But after a while I calmed down and we calmly discussed the matter. I think most people can speak dog if they concentrate on it.

He is a most curious animal. He runs sideways a lot. Why do puppies do that? I took him down to the pond this afternoon and threw him in and he turned fish instantly, flopping gloriously around in the foam, barking at the beavers, chasing imaginary shadows of his elders in sweeping, wet circles.

I laughed at him and he took my laughter as a caress and barked mindlessly at me, shaking the water off his gleaming back only to gurgle back into the water and come up a fish once more.

Is it possible for a man to love something of another species? I know that I miss loving, truly loving deeply, more than anything else. I felt some of that this afternoon. I walked back up to the house and got a towel and held the puppy in it, rubbing him dry and clean until I saw that he had fallen asleep in my arms.

I sat there with him like the canine madonna for nearly an hour, and in that time I counted eight different kinds of birds, and saw, for the first time, a pair of otters playing and chukking in the tall grass where the water ends.

July 20

Bill and I went into town today to buy dog food for Africa, and we settled on a fifty-pound bag of dry food and a dozen cans of wet food. I'll mix it to give his teeth time to harden.

Bill was talking about a deep-sea fishing trip he's going to take with his dad.

"We're going to Hilton Head this weekend," he said in his strong, even voice. "Then we're going all the way out in the Gulf Stream. It's a long ways. I hope we'll get some sail-fish, maybe even a marlin."

"I hope your luck holds, too."

"You can't imagine the thrill of big game fish," he said solemnly as we stood in line with the dog food.

"No, I can't," I said gravely.

"It's the kind of thing a man should do," he said. "Some way or other, you have to let people know you can do things on your own. I like being able to pull that kind of fish in and then having it mounted if it's big enough. It kind of makes you know you're not just a boy any more."

July 21

Quiet, terribly hot, dry. I read today there is nearly $4 billion worth of lost or buried treasure in the United States. That's only news for people like Bill McAdam.

Treasures. Buried. For God's sake.

July 22

Tuesday. I have been looking today at the trees in my yard. I am still amazed how trunks expand, how the space around them waits to be displaced.

I see the beech and the willow by the pond, and around the yard, water oaks and some pecan trees that have now expanded their canopy over the house, keeping it comfortable, despite the heat. The leaves are no longer tender, now into their season. There is also a sweet gum tree by the back door that has been here since I was a young boy.

Many of the pines are new and unexpected. I still remember the spaces between the trees as if I were a boy here many years ago. But the spaces between the trees and their shadows change each year, bending, spreading, turning the earth a different shade.

I walked along the edge of the pond and was lashed by the willow's drooping fronds, snake-green whips that whisper past you as you walk. When I turned, they were still moving, as if only part of me had come through and the rest were still whispering past.

July 23

Sometimes the far side of the pond seems to be in another time, gone foggy and hazy, indistinct and farther away the closer you look. Africa and I were napping this morning in the grass at the cool edge of Shadow Pond when I heard a soft kachunk of something plopping into the water. I sat for a moment and I thought I saw Willie standing silently on the far side of the pond with a slim frond of a fishing pole clutched in his hand. I stood and was ready to shout when I found I could no longer tell if it were Willie or merely some regal stand of cane, multicolored and wind-moving. I tried to stare at the spot, but it kept going out of focus. Africa did not awaken.

Finally, I called his name, but there was no movement there to betray him, and neither did the rod I took to be a pole sway an instant.

I listened for a long time, and I heard a hawk call as it curved over the pond heading for a field down the road.

July 24

Willie came back today. I was sitting on the front porch dozing when Africa began barking crazily, leaping backward in fits, his tail working, the black ears flat against his head. Willie was standing in a clearing between two white pines my Daddy planted, holding a stringer of fish in his hand. His face was as dirty as if he had been scuttling through a chimney.

I called to him and calmed the dog, but Willie only came forward a ways cautiously. Come on, he won't hurt you, I urged. Willie walked through the trees and slipped on to the porch. He held the stringer of catfish out to me and I took them.

"Let's cook and eat," I said. "You hungry?"

He gave no indication he understood me, and his demeanor reminded me of the time I had asked an exchange student from Hungary at Mt. Russell if he wanted to get some "chow." The boy looked at me suspiciously as if something were not clear. Willie looked at me that way.

We sat on the porch and I cut the heads off the cats and Willie skinned them with my pliers, flicking his thin wrists smoothly and ripping the tough, dark skin away from the white meat.

We washed them and I talked quietly to Willie about inconsequential things. He did not speak. I did not ask about the things he took and he gave no indication of contrition for the theft. We made batter and some hushpuppies and fried the fish in deep fat in the early afternoon.

He ate heartily and even polished off a bologna sandwich when we had peeled the last of the catfish from the bone. We went back on the porch after he helped me put the dishes in the sink.

I lit my pipe and tried to think of something to say, but his silence made it difficult, and each word sounded silly, tawdry against his terrible silence. His eyes frightened me, large, almost opalescent, as if afflicted with some retinal disease. Finally, after about half an hour, he stood and turned and looked at me with what seemed like a sort of passionate intensity. And then he was gone, his image lingering among the trees, the stringer dangling from his filthy hip pocket.

A teacher's trade is to talk and write. I am beginning to understand the dilemma of silence.

July 25

I ate lunch with Charles today and he remarked how well I look, but he said it with eyes that made it clear he feared for my future. I felt like a conspirator about Willie, but I could not bring myself to speak of him, even to Charles.

"Well, I guess you're sort of getting back to nature," he said.

"You know, that's kind of funny," I said. "I'm closer, but it seems I'm overwhelmed with all I can't remember."

"At least you knew once."

"Obviously not very well."

"But at least you knew."

That's how the talk went, mostly. Monosyllabic sometimes, of little consequence. I am damned tired of everyone trying to find some essential goodness in me because I'm old and dying.

If I were a Catholic, I'd burn some priest's ear.

July 26

Feeling fine today! I catalogued forty books before it got hot, and was delighted to find *The Sea around Us* by Rachel Carson, a first edition that Sara bought in New York City when we were visiting there in 1950.

I scanned the pages, wishing I had read it before I went to Savannah earlier this summer on my misadventure with Janet.

After the sun got flush on the land here, I went out with a hose and watered the beans that are now peeking through the ground. In the process, I watered myself down good. Africa wanted to be sprayed and he barked joyfully as we stood under the dripping fount in the hot sun.

Later, I did something I haven't done since I came back here: I went swimming in Shadow Pond. Africa came right alongside me, and once, when a beaver passed too near us, Africa howled in frustration at not being able to reach him.

I could live a long time like this.

July 27

I went to church in town this morning, and just as we finished "Come Thou, Fount of Every Blessing," a man's muttering argument with his son exploded into shouts that fixed everyone on the spot like a compass.

"You're not going to talk to me like that," the father thundered.

"You can just go to hell!" the young man screamed.

This is a proper church, and many of the older members were aghast, their mouths falling open in astonishment. But I noticed with amusement how the eyes of the young lit up, as if to prove within themselves that even in this sanctuary, life is more important than the pretension for one hour of being a bunch of pious ecclesiasts.

The young man dashed out, and the father turned stonily away from him.

"A disgrace," the father shuddered, looking straight ahead and almost in a stupor. "An absolute disgrace."

The preacher cleared his throat and acted as if nothing had happened and started reading the Scripture for the morning, reading, instead of the noted verses from Job, the Twenty-third Psalm.

An elderly woman humped in the pew a few seats from me trembled slightly for the rest of the service, but I could not tell if it was from moral outrage or Parkinson's disease.

July 28

I shaved, showered, and Old Spiced myself earlier this evening and took Callie over to Athens to see *Urban Cowboy*. Now, it is late as I write this at my table and drink a glass of cold milk. The pleasures of the senile.

We both thought the movie was awful, and I suppose I should have picked out something better, but I don't know one of these damn new movies from another. They don't make my kind of movie anymore. The lament of the elderly.

Now give me a movie like *Robin Hood* with Errol Flynn, or *Fighting Seabees* with John Wayne anytime.

I am as much an anachronism as the tolling of the bell in *Julius Caesar*. But *Urban Cowboy* is cheap trash.

Afterward, we went to a pizza place and drank beer and ate pizza, and some of the young people there stared at us lovingly. Callie and I had a good time, and I feel now there is something to our relationship, even though I will never tell her that. This kind of thing does not fit in with my plans.

I don't like being so threatened, but I am being blindly drawn toward anarchy, and at least on the fringes, there is something that does not make me afraid.

July 29

I am fascinated with the age to which certain people live. What determines how old a man will be when he dies?

Daniel Boone lived to be eighty-six; Mark Twain, seventy-four; Jefferson Davis, eighty-one; Thomas Edison, eighty-four; and so on. But how about Chatterton, Keats, and Shelley?

I suppose I will die next year, which will be in my seventy-sixth year. That seems all right with me. But seeing those dates that will be on my grave with some certainty is not pleasant or something on which I shall dwell.

July 30

I fear for Willie and wonder if I might be afraid of him, too. He is a wraith. I hear he has shown up once or twice at a distant relative's house, but that he hasn't been home. Why is no one worried about him?

I walked today in the woods for a long time looking for him, thinking I would run across him squatting beside a tree, but I found nothing, only an old campfire that probably was left by someone else.

I do not know how to act around children. I am used to the college-age person or the older man or woman. After Jim died, Sara and I didn't have the heart for talking about children and I am afraid something of that reticence is now bonded to my fear for Willie.

I am paralyzed when thinking about him. There must be something I can do.

July 31

It is night. Willie is here, sleeping on the couch, curled under a light sheet, shuddering with some dream. When I woke up this morning, I stood and stretched and looked down past the cottonwoods to the garden, and there he was, stalk-still, watering the garden. I tumbled into my jeans and dashed out without a shirt or shoes down to the garden and when he saw me, he smiled and waved, but he wouldn't talk.

I stood there for a long time, trying to get him to tell me where he had been and what he had eaten, but he grew sullen and began to get angry, so I took him by the arm, turned off the hose and led him back inside.

I cooked him thick, hickory-smoked bacon and eggs, as well as toast and grits and coffee. He ate a frightful amount, and I had to cook more eggs twice before he finally pushed himself away from the table.

He smelled terrible and his hair was matted and filthy. For all I knew, he had been stealing from people nearby, but I could not ask him. I made him strip on the front porch and get into the tub and scrub himself with hot, soapy water. He put on a shirt of mine and a pair of pants and tied them on with a short, soft rope.

He sat on the front porch all morning, reading an old issue of the *Saturday Evening Post* from the late '50s that I found. I told him to wait, that I would wash his clothes. He sat there in the warm sunshine.

For most of the day, he read and dozed and watched television. When suppertime came, I drove to a chicken place in town and got us a bucket. I ate a chicken breast and Willie ate the six pieces that were left, including most of a pint of potatoes and half a gallon of milk.

Now it is late and he is resting, sleeping, clean and silent. Why have I done this? His clothes are dry and stiff.

I am very tired. I am torn with his silence.

August 1

He is gone. I expected this. I did not expect to find a note that he left on the kitchen table, weighted with a half-empty bottle of maple syrup. Here is what it said:

> Mister Lackland, I am glad you fed me I am not hungary for a whiel no more. I take your bread and potoes. I will come back to see you sone. Willie.

I folded the note and slipped it into a decorated Japanese box I keep on the mantle. I decided to walk up to the Sullivan place after that to see if Willie was stopping by there or if they had heard from him.

The morning was hot and the drought continues. The air comes scuttling across the lake, almost picking up dust rather than moisture. I walked the mile through the woods toward the Sullivan place, feeling sweat trickling down my chest, but pleased at the stretching and swelling of my muscles.

His mother was standing in the front yard by a black pot of boiling peanuts, arms folded across her chest, looking like one of those photos Dorothea Lange took during the depression for the WPA. She looked at me suspiciously.

"Mrs. Sullivan," I nodded, taking off my old hat.

"Mr. Lachlan," she said, her voice throaty and deep.

"I just wanted to ask after Willie. He hasn't been by in a while." I felt this was no minor vice, lying to a child's mother, but my motives were jumbled and torn from logic and reason.

"He hasn't been here neither," she said. She smiled slightly. "If you see him, tell him not to come back none."

"How long has he been gone?"

"Since before my man died," she said.

"Where do you suppose he is?"

"Ain't got the foggiest. Don't care a whole hell of a lot. I mean him not even coming to the funeral and all." I put my hands in my pockets and cleared my throat.

"Can I tell him anything if he happens to come by my place? He does come by once in a while, or at least he used to."

"Yeah," she said. She walked up to me, too close, her leathered face right up in mine. *"Tell him his Ma said for him to go to hell."* She breathed hard, and I could smell her, an uncomfortable, dank, almost sweet smell. I backed up from her and turned and began walking away. I glanced over my shoulder after I'd gone about a hundred yards and she was still standing there, looking at me as I moved away.

Perhaps Willie was glad his father died. If he did, is her hate justified? Or is there some commandment that justifies the death of an evil man? Religion cannot clarify any of this for me. When I got home, I was terribly tired. I am going to bed early, though I took a nap and now I feel somewhat better.

My son. I write the words with a hand that trembles from age and fear and hope.

August 2

Out with the wildflowers again today. The weather is horribly hot, but I feel my skin acclimating to it, as if I were one of the seasonal animals of the forest.

Today I found a patch of lavender moss verbena *(Verbena tenuisecta)* alongside the road, small circles of crowns. The color gathered light around the flowers, the russet hues of red dirt behind all else for the eye to feast upon.

Lots of daisy fleabane, too. *(Erigon philadelphicus* L.).

The petals of the latter are surprisingly tough and resist being pulled off while they are young in their season.

August 3

How does one observe humanity? It is more difficult than studying the flaws of a mirror because each fissure in the glass leads always to the cast in the beholder's eye. There is no corollary for Willie Sullivan in the animal kingdom, therefore I study those creatures abstractly, in love with scale and fur. And pistils and stamens cannot reveal how terribly we treat our fellows and how pointless is the government to which we so nobly ascribe.

I could not bring myself to attend church today because I do not believe it would offer me any consolation for the mistrust I feel for the works of my own hands and heart.

August 4

It is important to die well. When Haydn was dying, Napoleon was bombarding the city of Vienna. A French bomb landed in the Kleine Steingasse where Haydn lay mortally ill. When the French forces occupied Vienna, a French officer visited Haydn and played on the composer's piano parts of Haydn's *Missa in Tempore Belli*. Near the end, later, Haydn got himself carried to the piano and played his national anthem, "Gott erhalte unseren Kaiser." Then he died.

An old man should be permitted a theatrical end if he chooses. Performers, public men should die with the drama they plan. Hubert Humphrey did this. But historians should be borne away by the dust on which they have built their dreams, shifting quietly into the past like the closing of an old and valuable book.

August 5

Worked most of the day on the paper about Fort Phil Kearny to be delivered in Sheridan on the twentieth. I am greatly pleased by this, and I have been organizing the speech to make it one of my best.

I suppose it is silly and indulgent to think this will be the crowning performance of a life of quiet study. And yet I am approaching it with some seriousness and with the feeling that what I say will make a difference to someone there, to those who will come after me. I would like to tell them not to specialize, to become broader each day, not deeper. And I would like to tell them that anyone who looks at what this country did to the Indians cannot possibly believe the jingoistic nonsense that has labeled us the land of the free and home of the brave.

We are a great country of narrow, mistaken old men who make laws that oppress us all. The only Americans who had freedom are now huddled on reservations that can only mirror our national greed, stupidity, and malignancy.

I will tell them that because it matters to me.

August 6

I took Bill McAdam with me to Atlanta today to do some research in the state archives building. Bill was a good companion, talkative, happy, full of good spirits. The sailfish he caught is being mounted and should arrive in a few weeks.

"It was like hooking a horse," Bill said, his eyes dancing as I drove. I could see him out of the corner of my eye, his hands moving as he talked. "Like a stallion. I held on until I could start taking some line in. It took half an hour to land him."

"How many times did he jump?" I asked. "I saw Spencer Tracy in *The Old Man and the Sea*."

"Well, that was a marlin, but this sailfish jumped eight times," he nodded.

"Must have been pretty," I said.

"Absolutely magnificent," Bill corrected.

He was very helpful, but I was anxious to get home before dark and so I left before I finished my work. When I got home, I found that Africa had torn the evening paper into thousands of pieces and part of Jimmy Carter's face had gotten stuck on the doormat. I left it there.

August 8

Quiet yesterday, today. Not feeling too well.

August 9

For some reason, I read Andrew Jackson's second inaugural address today. He said: "Let us exercise with forbearance and firmness. Let us extricate our country from the dangers which surround it."

I will write it here for myself: Andrew Jackson was a worthless son of a bitch and a liar.

August 10

I missed that yesterday was Izaak Walton's birthday, so after lunch today I went fishing in Shadow Pond. I did not attend church today.

I enjoy fishing more and more, despite the fact that the heat makes fish liable to bite less. I am now learning to tie trout flies, but I am much too impatient to make anything that would fool the trout. So I am content to trap the bluegill, bullhead, and largemouth with worms and crickets.

But the remarkable thing is what I caught today, early in the afternoon. I was idly watching the plastic bobber, feeling the warmth on my face when my rod nearly leapt from my hands and the line started whirring off. I was fishing with a fifteen-pound test line, but I thought I would soon go in with it or see it break.

I let it take out line, with visions of a monstrous bass. I worked him back in. Let him out. Worked him back in. Finally, he was worn and let himself be hauled to shore. Before he cut through the water, I knew what it was, not a shiny bass with its distended mouth, but a giant carp, its thick scales shining underneath the shallows.

I pulled it out. It was croaking like crazy, and I figured it weighed at least twelve pounds. Africa was shouting at it, hopping back every time it flopped in the grass. I cleared the hook from its mouth and nudged it back into the water. It hung for an instant, like part of a mobile, still, reconnoitering. And suddenly it was gone, so fast that you wondered if it were ever there.

I have had worse times along the banks of Shadow Pond.

August 11

Only ten days until Sheridan. Finishing up my paper, now polishing it. I haven't flown in some time.

I have been thinking more and more about Callie lately. I feel something for her, something deep. I think that it is only some old man's mild infatuation, but I remember what Thomas Jefferson wrote as an old man: "I find as I grow older that I love those most whom I loved first."

Should I invite her to go with me to Wyoming? Would that be all right? Would it offend her?

August 12

Andrew, you old lunatic, I'm right proud of you today. Here's what I did. I called Callie and asked her if I could come over and talk to her about something. I put on the Old Spice real good. This was essential. I was nervous. I drove over. I dallied as much as I could. I asked her to go to Wyoming. She grinned and looked down in her lap. I thought she was going to make fun of me.

"Well, why not?" she asked.

"Why not?" I repeated.

I said, of course, we would get separate motel rooms, and she looked at me with a smile in her eyes and nodded. This is really silly for people our age isn't it?

I asked her if she was afraid of people saying things, and she laughed out loud.

I am very happy about all this!

August 13

Willie came back early this morning and I finally lost my temper with him.

"Your mother would like to see you," I lied. "Where are you staying? What are you eating?" He sat on the sofa in front of me, his thin bones crossed sullenly. "I asked you a question." I said it insistently. He glared at me and started to get up, and I jumped across the room and grabbed him by the shoulders and knocked him back down.

"Damn you, talk to me," I thundered. He gulped and looked down.

"I don't never want to talk no more," he said defiantly.

"Well, that's just crazy," I said. "And answer my question. Where are you staying and how are you eating?"

"House down yonder about a mile, I reckon," he said, pointing southeast through the woods. I knew the spot, an abandoned frame house about half a mile off the lower end of the pond. "I'm eating me some fish and blackberries and stuff."

"Are you stealing?" I was starting to feel righteous.

"Yeah," he said looking at me fiercely.

"That's just great," I muttered. "You know I'll give you just about anything you want, but you're stealing. From me, too."

"I'm sorry."

"Really?"

"Not really."

I was mad as hell.

"You glad your Daddy died, Willie?"

"Do you think I am?"

"No, I don't think you are. But I think you're hurting." He looked at me with horror and shame, and his face quivered as if he would cry. I knew I had been right then, but his pain cut through my anger like a scythe cuts through fresh grass. Then he cried.

I put my arms around him. This was hard for me. And he cried on my shoulder, shaking. I fed him well and now he is asleep.

Who am I to lecture about lying? He knew I was lying about his mother and he told me he was never going back there. I'm afraid the welfare folks will find out about this. I'll ask Callie for advice.

August 14

There is a feeling that comes when you see someone cry, something that makes you want it to go on because it feels good to see someone hurt because it isn't you. You want them to regain composure quickly, but you forgive them, as you silently hope the tears will never stop, like a winter rain when you are inside by a fire. There is pain in crying but not in watching other people cry and there is more pain in trying to keep from crying when something terrible happens. There was one old man at Sullivan's funeral. His mouth trembled for a long time but he would not cry and I wanted to shake him and say go ahead and cry, there is nothing wrong with it, and I remembered how I cried over Sara and how nothing would make me stop for a long time and how everyone around me kept telling me to keep crying because it was good for me, when it was good for them, too. And so, when Willie cried last night, I held him to me so that he would see that I cared and cry some more because I did not want him to stop until I had enough.

August 15

Ordered the tickets today. I have finished the paper and re-typed it. I had forgotten how poorly I typed, and how Sara would always type my papers for me, slowly, patiently, rarely making mistakes. Oh, well. I do as I can.

Willie is still here, and I have been giving him books to read and he looks at them and tries to read them a little, but I have nothing so simple he can really understand it. We talked about history for a while today.

ANDREW: You ever heard of Napoleon, Willie?
WILLIE: He was a king, like, I think.
ANDREW: Do you know when he lived?
WILLIE: Bible times, I imagine.
ANDREW: What country did he live in?
WILLIE: That was before they had those.

And so on. I sat him down and told him the story of Napoleon, and he sat there looking down across the pond, chewing on a tuft of broom sedge, nodding sometimes as if he understood.

August 16

The garden is dying. The beans have dropped their stems, the pods clutched up from drought and heat. It is nearly unbearable. I can't count the times it has been over 100 this summer. Several times, sweating on my bed, I thought it was time for me to meet my maker. I'll tough this damned weather out because too much is going on now.

But with all the heat, there is still, at night, the marvelous haze of soft stars spread like a comforter across my home. I sit under the canopy of willows by the pond sometimes on these hot nights and wonder why I have lived so long, as if a man chooses rightly to die. But I think less of dying now. Sometimes, when I have sunken into a reverie under Orion, I listen to the pumping of my heart and I know that each breath has its beauty, just as each wing has its perfect trace along the august face of the heavens.

August 17

Went to church in town today with Callie and people looked
at us like they look at people. Callie didn't care and I didn't.
At one point during the sermon, a boring treatise on the rolling away of the rock in front of Jesus' tomb, one young boy,
about ten, I guess, burst out laughing. He was sitting next to
another boy I took for his brother. No one really minded except for the boys' mother, who turned crimson and shot
them a stern glance.

I thought for the rest of the hour how well I like laughter
from young people. In teaching my classes at Mt. Russell, I
always told jokes to make the studies more fun, and the students seemed to like that.

Nothing is so serious or profound that the right person
can't change pompous sobriety into mirth.

August 18

Willie has gone again. This time, he left no note, but I know
I will see him again because he is finally talking to me. I still
feel strange at keeping my relationship with him a secret,
but I have promised I will talk about it to Callie on the way
out.

Callie. I see her face in everything, even washing dishes.
Make a fool of yourself, old man. It's all right now. Her
eyes, her hands, the gentleness of her words. Will she still
be around in a year? Will I? I'll live not farther away than a
few days because I know what awaits us all at that distance,

and the times now seem to be wrapping me in a new and loving warmth.

August 19

We are over Kansas, whispering across the Plains. I can see them stretched out below us. Callie was cold and put her sweater over her chest and was soon asleep. I kept hoping her head would find its way to my shoulder, but so far, it hasn't. I am writing this quietly so as not to awaken her. The trip has been lovely, if a man can use that word.

Later. She was awakening when I last wrote. We finally made it here to Sheridan, and we are staying at a motel. The weather is much cooler than in Georgia, a delight. We were met by Alfred Hudson, one of those in charge of the conference, and he told me when I would speak, tomorrow at about 2 P.M. I was astounded and nonplussed to find my visit had been played up by the local press on the front page, mainly because, as they note, I am an expert on Fort Phil Kearny, but also, I suspect, because it is a slow news week. I was also staggered to hear they expect a couple of hundred people to attend my speech.

Callie and I had supper in a steakhouse and we talked of many things but I could not bring myself to tell her of Willie for some reason. I thought it would be unfair now to both of us. Maybe on the flight back. I wanted to tell Callie some things, but I could not say them, dishonest with her and perhaps myself even at this age and distance from the fumbling lover I always was.

But we went into a bar and had drinks afterward and stayed up too late and when I took her to her room, I kissed her on the cheek and she turned to me and smiled.

"Oh, for heaven's sake, Andrew," she said. And she grabbed my cheeks and kissed me on the mouth. I kissed her back and we stood there in the doorway for a long time, listening to the night.

August 20

Speech went well.

I won't write what Callie said or how it came about, but we are going to sleep together tonight. This is far more important than the speech.

Now it is late afternoon, and I am sitting here under the whir and groan of my air conditioner, pleased with my successes, and how much I enjoy things now and what a misery it is to think that it will not last forever.

But I feel fine, and I wonder sometimes if there was a mistaken diagnosis that led them to tell me what they told me, and maybe that I could live another twenty years and find out what will happen to old men then.

I can't concentrate on my speech. I just think of Callie and what she said and how pleased I am. And that this all matters a great deal, and that history is only a gauze over my next breath, a gauze I love but cannot bear forever. Too much that I have seen is now pressed only like a flower between the pages of a book.

August 21

She asks what I am writing in these pages and I say that it's my journal and it is too private to let her read and she smiles and says she understands that. She is wearing a chiffon peignoir and her hair is down over her shoulders. I cannot understand how skin is so smooth and perfect. Perhaps I overlooked something.

It is morning, a lazy morning, and no one is in my room and we have spent the night in each other's arms, her hand resting slightly on my chest. I told her I should speak to the management about the creaking bed and she laughed and told me I was a silly old man. She's right, of course. I don't give a damn.

We are going out for breakfast. It has been impolitic to speak of love.

August 22

Tired, back home in Georgia, but full of piss and vinegar. On the way back I told her about Willie and asked her what I should do.

"Are you uncomfortable around him?" she asked.

"Very."

"Does he help you do things around the house?"

"Never."

"Do you feel sorry for him?"

"Not particularly."

"Do you think he's really been stealing?"

"Yes." (Why did I admit this?)

"Will you call the sheriff?"

"No."

"What will you do then?"

"I don't know."

She commiserated and said she could not understand why I had gotten messed up in this. Then we talked about my illness and I told her how good I feel and that I'll live a long time, but she was worried about me not taking the treatments.

I drove her home and we walked inside and I held her in my arms for a long time and we kissed and I told her I didn't know what I was going to do without her around.

"Let's rest for a couple of days and then talk about it," she said.

"Okay," I said.

What are the alternatives? Marriage? Living together? Dating? Perhaps I could get married again, but I do not think she would choose that alternative.

I am in love with Callie McKenzie, and I write that at peril of losing my absorption in my own tears.

August 23

It has been ten days since I saw him, so I decided to walk to the house where he said he was staying. The woods are clogged with weeds and wildflowers, camphor weed, and Queen Anne's lace, and I walked rapidly south around the pond until I got near the place and found a trail. When I was a boy, a family of Browns lived in that house, white trash who made moonshine and got their first cousins pregnant.

I came through the woods and up to the house. It is now half-gulped by the kudzu and leaning crazily, as if it would fall at the urging of a gentle breeze. I listened. Nothing. A blue jay, screaming, the low hoot of a mourning dove. When I got nearer the house, I could hear low, urgent voices. I stopped and turned my head slightly. There. What were they saying?

I crept closer, my rubber-soled shoes moving softly through the dust. The sound was coming from a frameless, paneless window. I knew those sounds. Love making, grunting, the slight slapping of flesh, the soft curse of pleasure. I leaned against the house, not knowing what to do. The window was just over my head, so I leaned and went past it quickly, but my voyeuristic tendencies asserted themselves and I walked around to the back, on which the room also fronted. I leaned and took a quick glance into the room, leaned back out again.

I could tell it was Willie by his hair. He was lying on top of a girl who appeared to be very young, short, lithe. They were bucking at each other wildly. My stomach churned. There on that dirty mattress. Why did this have to be, in this filth here in a sunken house?

I was torn between shame and pleasure, an almost unbearable combination, I believe. I crept away quickly, looking sometimes over my shoulder to see if he had heard me and was now looking out. But I could only hear the curses grow louder from both of them. Those curses.

I got home very tired and disturbed and I don't care if I ever see Willie Sullivan again.

August 24

Went with Callie to church. I could not tell her about what I saw yesterday, but I am no longer so angry and cannot tell why I was so angry. I wonder who the girl was and if she might get pregnant. How terrible that would be, for Willie to make this girl pregnant and with nothing to give her. Would he bring her to my house, the girl and the baby, for black-eyed peas and cornbread when the weather gets cold?

August 25

Willie came back today, and he appears to have put on some weight. We went fishing at the pond, but they weren't biting and we caught nothing. He seemed more cheerful than usual, and he does not know I know why.

WILLIE: I'd like to catch me a big ol' catfish.
ANDREW: Where are you going to live when it gets cold?
WILLIE: *(Ignoring me.)* When they get big enough, you can get filets *(he pronounced* fill-ets) off 'em. Fry 'em up with corn meal. You know how.
ANDREW: You can't live in that house when it's cold.
WILLIE: It ain't cold now.
ANDREW: But it will be getting cold in a month or two.
WILLIE: It ain't cold now.
ANDREW: You're going to freeze your little butt off, Willie.
WILLIE: *(Smirking.)* I'll stay warm.
ANDREW: *(Hoping he will fess up.)* What have you got to keep you warm?
WILLIE: A warmer. *(He laughs. I do, too.)*
ANDREW: What's that?

WILLIE: I was tellin' you about catfish.
ANDREW: *(With resignation.)* Yes, I remember that. I remember that.

August 26

It is night now. I miss the rain terribly. My house lacks something, curves, corners perhaps. I am meeting Callie tomorrow to talk. I listen to the frogs coughing their rituals in the darkness.

August 27

Something is wrong. I knew it. She sat quietly on the sofa, almost regal, looking at the wall over my shoulder when she talked to me, or rather, at me. As best as I remember, this is what we said.

"I don't think it would be wise for us to continue this relationship," she said. I sat in an overstuffed chair facing her.

"Why not?" I asked.

"I'm too old for this sort of thing," she sighed.

"That's ridiculous."

"No. It's the truth now. I do feel something for you but there is no way I can do anything but hurt you."

"You sound like a high school sophomore and you think I'm one, too. What are you talking about?"

"Don't get huffy."

"I'm not getting huffy."

"You were too getting huffy." She nodded her head for emphasis.

"I'm sorry," I said, restraining myself, "Could you please tell me what I have done to offend you?"

"Nothing, nothing," she pleaded. "But please believe that there is nothing to be gained by our continuing this relationship."

"I can't believe that."

"Anyway, it's so."

We talked for a while longer, but nothing came of it. I got back home angry, flushed, not knowing what had happened or why. Human conduct is an eternal Rosetta Stone to me, and I have no hopes of deciphering it.

I took a walk with my dog, but it didn't make me feel much better.

August 28

I am resting here in my ruins. How terrible it is to love someone who does not care for you. Nothing is more desolate than the feeling of someone turning away from your caresses as if you were no more than a cold wind whistling down from the north in the winter. I cannot beg someone to love me, but I ask it without hope these days. There is some dignity left in me, but it has fallen down where even the shadows fail.

August 29

Okay, then.

I busied things up today and had a most interesting time of it. I climbed carefully into the old well, the one Daddy built when we moved here, and rescued a turtle, two salamanders and a newt from the well's mossy bottom. It is about seventeen feet down there, I judge, and while I was down, I had a vague hope that it would collapse and smother me into the rich coolness of the earth. But then I looked up over me as I lingered and I saw the hazy blue summer sky, and the studied arc of a Cooper's hawk, and I knew that I would rise from the earth and walk among other living things.

Down in the well, there is a pervading dampness and several different kinds of mushrooms and mosses which I cannot catalog. The turtle was a box terrapin, obviously with no business in there. When I climbed back up the jagged rocks, I gently set the box on the ground and it was a full five minutes before the fellow poked his head out and inhaled the hot forest air.

I was almost immediately stricken with the idea that he had been cool and well-fed and that I had placed him again at the convenience of his enemies. I am amazed at how many thoughtless acts of good will pass each day without complaint from the victim.

August 30

Saturday. School has started back and Bill McAdam came by this morning, pleased to tell me what he is studying in biology and history, his two favorite courses. He also plays on the football team in the defensive backfield, I believe, and he is very proud of this.

"For my first experiment, I'm going to test the effect of external stimuli on unicellular organisms," he said.

"Really? What does that entail?" I asked. He ducked his head with some embarrassment.

"I'm going to put various chemicals on amoebas and see how long they live."

"What will that prove?"

"Which substances kill them fastest."

"Why do you want to know that?"

"Well . . . I think it would . . . well, just as research, you know."

I thought the idea preposterous, but I didn't say so, and he was obviously hurt that I found no enthusiasm for his project. But I did talk football with him.

I told him the fishing would be improving this fall at the pond, and he smiled and said maybe he'd try that, maybe he would, because bobber fishing is more fun than they say.

Than they say.

August 31

I could not bring myself to go to church this morning, not in town because I didn't want to see Callie and not anywhere else because I am not in a particularly good mood with the Almighty at the present time.

I find that as each month ends, I am not as joyous as the month before, and that I can mark what I have forgotten and lost more easily than what I have learned and gained.

The drought and heat have completely killed my garden. The vines are wizened, brown, turned with their hulls to the blistering sky. Shadow Pond is so low that the mosquito problem has gotten worse in the marshy mud left by the receding water.

I walked up to Amos Crick's house this afternoon, but he was in bed with some kind of ailment and his wife wouldn't let me in. I chatted with her for a moment and forgot any idea about seduction because she is bloated and she has stray hair on her chin.

And yet autumn will come with its lovingly crafted death for all things, and I will inhale deeply when the cool air comes and dream of the histories that follow me into another season.

September 1

The healing does not begin within you. It swells down from the tulip poplars and up from the galax scattered on the forest floor, and it rises from the singing of crickets in the early morning.

I feel it growing in me, the knitting again of my old swaying bones, the gentle assurance of open spider lilies and the common wind making metronomes of the cattails.

I have never lived by excess in the autumn, rather breathing more deeply when I walked from my house to classes, breathing in the fragrance of the small smokes of autumn and hickory and ash. And I would watch the birds ascending and leaving, knowing they would come back, those who flew well where they must fly.

And the colors masked by chlorophyll would spread into the leaves, and I would stand there at the crest and watch random clusters float past me, and I would know then in which season I had rested and when the healing begins.

September 2

I began surveying Shadow Pond today. I decided to wait until winter, but this seems cowardly to me, and when I would be least likely to be among the animals there.

The pond is, I have read, about 250 acres, really more of a lake—in fact a large lake. I own more than three-fourths of it from the northern end nearly to where it narrows and changes into the Cohatchee River. I have never posted the land, and people know they are welcome to fish, though I have met hunters and let them know they are not welcome.

I drove to the northern end of the pond this morning and parked along a fence line put up by a man to whom I rent land for grazing. He has rented this land for his Holsteins for nearly thirty years, renting it from my mother before her death.

I parked and walked through the stubble-grazed field until I came to the woods through which I could find a place where three creeks join to form the pond. I played along here as a child, racing my horse downhill at a gallop until we splashed into Edison Creek, then across it and up the next hill like an Indian.

I took graph paper, but I didn't know what I was doing. This is a human survey of the shoreline, I decided, not a geographic survey. I walked along the edge of the pond, tracing the curves of the shore on paper, writing in words sometimes, like "small beech" or "granite outcropping."

I took Africa with me and once, when some ducks came skidding into the water, he took off after them, but soon found himself alone in the middle of the pond and so he came out, tired and wet. But he was soon perky again, and we spent two hours walking around before I got tired and we went back to the car.

Now, I am very tired and will sleep.

September 5

Very sick for two days. From the hike? I thought yesterday one time I was dying. Perhaps it will come soon.

I am not ready.

September 6

I have decided it was a virus of some kind, because today I am much stronger. I will spend the day resting, though, because I want to get strong again.

September 7

Callie called me last night and asked me to meet her for church this morning, which I did. Instead of going inside for church, we sat in my car and she cried for a long time.

"I know I hurt you," she said.

"You don't have to do this," I said. I felt great. I wanted her to cry and apologize and now, at this slight distance, I feel guilty and angry at my arrogance.

"You don't understand," she said. "I've been doing this my whole life. I did it all the time with my husband, and I did it before we married and after he died. I can't make a commitment. I have to control everything in my life. I cannot bear not being able to create my own order."

"I'm not sure I believe in order anymore," I said. I looked around us to see if anyone were looking. We were alone in the crowded parking lot. The car was very hot.

"Nor I," she said. "There's no sense in planning anything for your life when all your plans turn out to be ashes."

"Your life hasn't been in ashes," I said.

"Please just don't hate me," she said. I felt sick for feel-

107

ing superior, and I moved closer to her and took her in my arms and she put her head on my shoulder.

"I don't hate you," I said, but I felt different. She said she would call me in a few days, and I kissed her on the cheek.

My health seems to be improving steadily.

September 8

This journal is getting thick. What is the purpose of all these thousands of words? Moving toward something? Away from it? It is finer to be taught than to teach, and it is finer to think about trees than ideas.

September 9

Willie is back, and he wants to know if he can move in with me. He talks quickly now, with confidence. I am afraid of what I am doing.

I think I have a good ear for conversation. I like to write it down as I remember it and have been doing it for years. But Willie talks so fast now that I cannot catch it all. Once today when he talked, it sounded something like this: "It's got skeetos down 'ar so thick they damn near carry you off and when they bite it hurts awful bad, and they bit me right on the rear end when I was sleeping with no clothes on, and I jumped up and swatted 'em, but they kept on coming until I started screaming, see, and running out into the woods and they won't follow there, if you get far enough away from water."

That's what it sounded like, though it is probably imprecise. I had to ask him this.

"Did you ever have a girl down there with you?" I said it plainly, matter-of-factly. His mouth curled down, and then he looked up at me, right into my eyes.

"I ain't seen nobody but you this summer." I wanted to shake him and tell him I knew he was lying, but the words would not come, and I nodded stupidly and told him he could stay with me as long as he chooses.

There is a whisper of fall here today, but it is still hot.

September 10

Willie, Africa, and I went up to the north end of the pond at dawn this morning and worked our way down the eastern side, mapping and making notes. Willie was cheerful and alert. Last night, I scrubbed his hair with strong shampoo. Then I sat him on the front porch with a towel over his thin shoulders and snipped off a good deal of his hair with my kitchen scissors. I drew his foot off on a piece of brown paper. Then I drove into town and bought him some new blue jeans, and shirts and a pair of heavy boots that will do this winter. The boots fit well enough.

Now, Willie looks remarkably better, and I am rather vain about my handiwork.

He asked good questions while we were noting landmarks, and he laughed and played with Africa. When we got home, I felt wonderful and relaxed, almost as if I had done nothing but rest all day in bed and dream of a land of milk and honey.

September 11

Today, I am planning a course of study for Willie. I told him I would teach him and he reluctantly agreed. I have heard that his mother told the school's visiting teacher that Willie moved to her sister's house in Virginia. I cannot forgive that terrible woman for this treachery, but I understand it.

The real challenge is in seeing at what point he has arrived in his education. While Willie spent the day fishing, I began a list of "challenges" that should give me an idea of his educational abilities.

Since I have little expertise in mathematics, I stopped by the bookstore in town and bought a book on rudimentary math that should help me prepare. I will teach him for three hours a day, in the morning. That should be adequate. Then, for an hour after lunch, we will study nature together.

Perhaps I will call him William.

September 12

My mother was terribly afraid of storms. As a girl living on the plains of Oklahoma, she saw tornadoes many times, and she learned their destructive power. I remember how she would take us into the cellar when bad storms came. That cellar, which is directly under the den here, was dug out by my father when he built the house and has been used for storage now for years.

As a precaution, I have decided to clean it out as a room for Willie. When I told him about it, his eyes grew large and he seemed utterly delighted by the plan. We moved all the furniture off the den floor and then the heavy rug. I didn't suppose the cellar had been opened for many years. I have not touched it since I moved back here, and I doubt my mother opened it for years before her death.

I got my extension light with a 200-watt bulb and dropped it into the small room. It is about ten feet square. Lizards and other small feet flashed around the walls when the light hit. To my amazement, it had been cleaned out except for one old, moldering trunk. It is brick lined, but cracks had appeared here and there.

"Look at that place," Willie exulted.

"I'm afraid there's no light in it," I said.

"You don't need no light at night," he shrugged. "It's all dark."

"And we can get a heater so it won't be cold this winter."

"Okay by me," he nodded.

The steps are still as firm and hard as the day my father laid them there seventy-five years before. We went down. The odor was that of old clothes, musty, and seemingly dry and wet at the same time.

In the trunk were a few old books, nothing of much interest, some clothes and such, but one thing touched me deeply. It was a letter from my father to my mother, dated December 25, 1899, before they were married. It was short. Here is what it said:

My Grace, This bright day of our Lord will, I hope, find you safe and warm in your parents' home. This has been a fetching season for us and I come to this celebration with the certainty that I have from you the same affection and love I give. Yours, Charles Lachlan.

September 13

A fine Saturday. I spent the day working on a syllabus for Willie while he swept out the cellar and disinfected it, patching the faulty brick work. Now, Willie is sleeping in the bed with me, but I have come to enjoy my nocturnal solitude and will be grateful when he moves. He is tremendously excited by his new room. After work on the syllabus, we drove to Covington and bought a single bed, a lamp, bedside table, a small rug, and a radio.

"Your grandad getting all this for you?" the sales clerk asked.

"Yeah, he is," Willie said.

We will spend tomorrow working on his room. School starts on Thursday, September 18.

September 14

Callie has not called me and for some reason I do not expect her to. I am contented with Willie here now, full of plans and energy, and I wonder what compulsion pushed me toward Callie in the first place.

Since I cannot take Willie to church, I insisted that we have a small service here at the house. We went east into the woods and sat under a large cedar tree in which a mockingbird trilled and clicked constantly.

I read the story about Moses striking the stone, and I asked Willie if he had ever heard of that, but he hadn't, so I explained it to him. He seemed to be ignoring me.

"Are you thinking about what I'm telling you?" I asked.

"I killed one of them mockingbirds one time," he said.

"Why?"

"I wanted to cut open his mouth and see what made it sing so many different things."

"Did you find out?"

"Naw."

"No, *sir*."

"No, sir, I didn't. Just bird guts. That was all. They just sing different songs."

"Maybe God made them that way," I suggested.

"That don't matter," he shrugged. "Birds just do what they do. You watch 'em. That's all it is."

I allowed as how I knew little more about it than anyone else does.

September 15

We began getting his room ready yesterday and we finished it up today. I am startled at how good it looks. The room is now cozy, rather than crowded and small, and because it is in the earth, it is by far the coolest place in the house. Likewise, it should not be unbearably cold this winter, though I will buy a space heater for it.

As a final touch, I hung (with some difficulty since the walls are brick) a portrait of Napoleon that was painted by a student of mine at Mt. Russell and given to me as a gift.

Willie looked at it a little suspiciously, but he is ready to indulge in any whim I might have.

September 16

It is finally starting to get a little cooler. If I have loved in my life, if I have loved only words and stories and histories and then Sara, perhaps now I love something else because I have lived long enough for it to come to pass.

September 17

I have discussed my syllabus with Willie and he is politely diffident. I cannot tell for certain what his educational level might be, so my selections may be arbitrary and in need of modification.

We will work on fractions in math, Indians in history, sentence construction and grammar in English, short stories in literature. Our biology work will be confined to our nature walks. We have informally agreed on this.

I asked him how he felt about hiding like this and he said it was better than living at home and that he was happy here with me. I asked him to write me a page about how he felt, and although his literacy level is low, he expresses himself all right. I am convinced that he can expand himself and be a reasonable, well-educated young man.

September 18

First day of classes. We studied the lessons on the back porch. I have never taught like this. It is so personal that it is hard to believe that there are issues other than each other's integrity. There is no dignity in teaching this way, but it is the way I have chosen to help Willie.

Our nature walk went well, and I told Willie about my search for wildflowers, and he showed me some rabbit tobacco and rolled it into a cigarette that we both tasted. I thought it was terrible.

I was not prepared for what he wanted to discuss after we got back. I am still uncomfortable about such things, though I tried to be honest.

WILLIE: You think girls like bigger peckers better?
ANDREW: Why would you ask that?
WILLIE: You're teaching me, ain't you?
ANDREW: That's right.
WILLIE: Well?
ANDREW: I guess they do. I don't know. How would I know?
WILLIE: I figured you been around.
ANDREW: Not nearly so much as you might think. I was married to the same woman for forty-seven years, Willie.
WILLIE: Oh. She's dead?
ANDREW: That's right.
WILLIE: I just heard girls like bigger peckers better.
ANDREW: Does that bother you?
WILLIE: *(Brightening.)* Me? No. not me.

September 19

I am a cowardly slob. I called Callie this afternoon after Willie and I finished our lesson and she was warm and cheerful and wanted to see me. As soon as I hung up, I realized that I had made a mistake, that I really no longer wanted to be involved with her.

But it's no good. I will meet her tomorrow night at her place for dinner. I am relieved and angry that I have sold my pride for a little comfort.

September 20

I have spent most of this day in misery. Willie went off and said he wouldn't be back until Monday. What can I do with him? I am as terrified of his leaving as of his staying. There is no comfort for me when I get closer to people than things. I would be better lecturing about Red Cloud to the migrations of geese than trying to hold Willie close to me, as if he were moved by something as lovely as blood.

Tonight, I am going to Callie's, and that will also probably end miserably. This is a terrible day.

September 22

It is late afternoon as I write this. Willie came back as he said he would, and while the morning was warming around us, we talked of history and nouns and verbs, and he wrote it all down and asked good questions. Now, it is hot again, and I am smoking my briar and puzzling about how Callie took me to her Saturday night and moved us away from the sofa to the bed.

It is possible, I suppose, that this has been her pattern for life, casually coupling with her latest interest. I hear there are such women, though I have been so naïve as to believe nothing of the debauches that take place in my imagination.

But perhaps she does feel something for me, feeling what she proclaimed, love, the desire to hold me until there was nothing left of this world but the sun and our dust. And yet she knows I am a querulous old man whose final days have already been printed on the calendars to come. And she takes that also to her breast and tells me she will hold me until then.

Now, it is my turn to be coy, to tell her that I must retreat to my solitude and think of what it would mean and how best we can consecrate this creaking friendship she calls love.

I have not told her about my new arrangement with Willie, and it seems to me that her inbred sense of propriety will not allow her to accept such a thing without guilt. And if I should accept her warmth and sex, do I risk sharing with her my disorder and so bring it upon her?

I sit here with the sun streaming through the window and hear Willie shouting at Africa as they swim in the marshy edge of Shadow Pond. And I feel my love moving softly among names I have known for too little time.

September 23

"Is a proverb a part of an active verb or one of them passive verbs?" Willie asked.

"Very funny."

"No, I mean it. What does that mean?"

"I'm not going to fall for that old joke."

"It ain't no joke. I want to know."

I quit laughing and started telling him seriously and when I got totally lost in trying to make sense, his face screwed up into a laugh and he started choking with glee. I laughed, too, though I was not delighted in being gulled by my only student.

I told him about the Ghost Dance during our history session, and his face told me that he may now believe there is a new earth, one that will come when the white man finds an end to his stupidity and greed and ignorance and vengeance.

September 24

In thinking about Callie, I have been ill at ease recalling Sara because in my mind she is growing less than sacred, though still far more than profane. I keep trying to remember something terrible I did as a young man and the feeling washes me like these early autumn winds. I gulp the past the way a fish out of water gulps the air, desperately, mindlessly, almost as if it no longer mattered anyway. What agony comes from such painful duality!

It wasn't always so great for Sara and me and I write that with hands that are as unsteady as a moth in a rising wind. I have fictionalized our past, moved all those years of benign indifference into one moment under the linden trees when we were young and very much in love.

I detest myself for writing these things.

September 25

For every man who sees truly, there are a dozen thinkers. If I write *Passiflora incarnata*, I see the purple-fringed crown of the passionflower, not some dusty language stretched upon the page.

I will try to see truly. I am tired of contemplation and reflection, but one cannot change methods when the study is nearing its end.

Things are happening around me now. I will put this journal upon the table and see to them.

September 26

When Bill McAdam came over today, I had to get Willie to hide in the cellar. When I told Willie to go down, he looked at me as if I had betrayed him to the enemy. That hurt, but I felt too vulnerable.

While Bill and I were above him talking about Mohandas K. Gandhi, Willie had a sneezing fit that sounded strange, muffled through a handkerchief. Sometimes, it sounded like someone moving furniture around down there.

Bill has become obsessed with assassinations and the execution of the guilty.

"The guy who shot Gandhi, um, that was on January 30, 1948, was named Godse," Bill said, tracing his thoughts with his eyes.

"I remember well when it happened," I nodded. "Didn't remember his name, though."

"Then on November 15, 1949, they hanged him and another guy who was a conspirator. It took Godse fifteen minutes to strangle."

"That's awful."

"You think that's bad? The guy who shot McKinley? They poured sulphuric acid over him after they electrocuted him. That was on October 29, 1901."

"Why did you memorize those dates?" I asked, puzzled. (Why did *I* memorize them as he spoke?)

"I don't know," he said with a smile. "For the fun of it, I guess."

September 27

It is Saturday, so Willie and I are not having school today. He was very angry about having to hide when Bill came over, and he wanted to know about Bill so I told him.

"He's the son of a guy I know," I said. "He's been coming over to visit me off and on this summer."

"Then he's like me," Willie said darkly.

"Well, he comes to see me."

"He don't live here like I do."

"No, he lives with his folks. He's a couple of years older than you, Willie."

"He lives with his mama and daddy?"

"That's right."

"Okay."

We drove to Athens early in the afternoon and went bowling. I had not been bowling in years, and it was the first time Willie had ever set foot in the place. I showed him how to hold the ball, but for the first game, he kept throwing it in the gutter.

After three games, though, he broke 100 and wound up beating me. He was delighted with himself and I took him out to eat after. On the way home, his ebullience faded a little and he silently watched the cattle in the sunburned fields.

September 28

Callie and I met this morning at her house and took a walk back a few streets through the town cemetery. It is a place full of shifting shade, neatly trimmed plots and sudden gaudy pink shafts beside restrained granite rectangles. I have always loved walking in cemeteries. At Mt. Russell, Sara and I would walk sometimes through the large graveyard, reading epitaphs on older stones. Nobody does that anymore. I suppose it would be thought overemotional.

Our hands fumbled together as we passed the last resting place of Frederick Woodson Branton (1782–1860), founder of the town, at least the one with the money and the staying power. He does have an epitaph: "Farmer, congressman, man of peace, inventor, father and husband." In that order, no doubt. I never heard what he invented.

"It's so peaceful here," she said. Several blocks away, the church bells were lazily tolling in the cool air.

"It's kind of like a feeling you can't hear," I suggested.

"Yes. Like his voice." She was pointing at the grave stone of her mother and father and a wave of tenderness and pity swept over me. She was dressed in an old-fashioned dress, one with a collar that looked too high, a little loose around the ankles.

"I don't guess we ever forget, do we," I said.

"Never," she whispered. We moved on, our grip becoming tighter.

"What do you want from me?" I asked. She did not look at me.

"Friendship," she said. "Love. I don't know. That. Something."

"Why did you send me away?"

"Why haven't you called me?"

"Do you always answer a question with another question?"

"Don't you?" She was smiling and so was I but we could not talk about our relationship any more. We sat under a chestnut tree and listened to the voices of morning among the stones.

September 29

Things have taken a dangerous turn. I got a call this morning from the sheriff who asked me if I ever saw William Sullivan out around my place. I gulped and chewed on the question.

"Not since his daddy died," I said firmly.

"Well, we're looking for him. His Ma told us that he was up north with her sister but we had that checked out and he's not there. So we had to declare him missing."

"Sorry I can't help you," I said.

"If you see him over there, let us know," he said.

"I will," I said.

I sat for a long time on the back porch looking down the slope through the pine woods. I took Willie on our nature walk today, but the whole time I was anxious and not looking for flowers.

September 30

I left Willie at the house after our lessons and walked up to Amos Crick's house. He was sitting on the front porch whittling and spitting.

"There was a baby born in Melrose with two heads last week," he said before I could say anything.

"That's awful," I said.

"A real monster, I'll tell you. Said one head had this wild look, and it was alive and the other was real peaceful and it was dead."

"I don't believe that. That's sick."

"Hell, man, it's true," he said. "Said this nigger midwife took one look at it and screamed her head off that it was the devil and left it hanging out of the mother. A monster was all it was. Two-headed monster."

"Why do you repeat those old stories?"

"I like to see people's faces when they hear bad things."

"What for?"

"Tells you a lot about folks, how they look."

"I think you're crazy, Amos."

"I won't argue that. No sir. How could I argue that?"

October 1

I am sitting in the boat, drifting as the afternoon drifts around me, full of the high colors of early fall and the sounds of leaves scratching off their summer wax. The boat keeps turning in the same direction, the bow acting as a mobile pivot, always the turning point, but moving gently along. I am not fishing today.

My knees hurt today. Arthritis? I rest this book on them as I write, feeling something moving too far in the joints.

Last night I dreamed of the two-headed baby that Amos Crick talked about. The living head was Willie and he was talking about Napoleon and Wellington and the other head looked like Bill McAdam, but not quite. It was bluish and its crown rested on the neck of the other head.

When I awoke, I was breathing too hard and I think I called out. But I heard nothing, only the crickets scraping their songs in the damp grass.

And so today I am of these two minds, half ready to spread and conquer with a roar, half ready to curl peacefully under a tree and breathe lightly until there was no reason to breathe any longer.

October 2

I took Willie to Sears in Athens and we bought a tent and sleeping bags and a Coleman stove and lantern. I have promised him that we will go camping in the mountains this weekend.

I feel quite good about this. No one will know us there.

October 3

I am pleased beyond praise with the progress Willie is making with his studies. His reading has already noticeably improved, as have his diction and vocabulary. He is asking good questions and working hard and I have been curious about the whole affair and feel rather like a character in *Pygmalion*. Is some myth behind me, driving me toward this intensity?

To reward him, I bought him a pump BB gun. He has spent the afternoon destroying tin cans behind the house. I tried it, but I have defective eyesight and missed most of the time.

Tomorrow, we are leaving at dawn and driving into the mountains of western North Carolina to camp for two nights. We are gathering our food and necessities tonight.

This is as good as Christmas, Willie said, except I never had that many good Christmases.

October 4

There is darkness here, though nothing is still: motion around me. I am sitting close to my lantern, the wick turned high, throwing an orange corona around our campsite. It is past midnight, and all the other campers in the small campground on the river have gone to sleep. Willie is curled inside his sleeping bag.

This was the country of the Cherokees before they were driven out. When I hear the gulping of the river and the moving wings of the night birds, I think of Indians.

But now, alone with pen noises and the hissing of moths as they die on the lantern's globe, I also think of time, and how it cradles my weaknesses and failures with benevolence and even charity. Nothing is planned in terms of time: before the next word, before the next syllable, something has changed everything.

Still, there is goodness here among the rumors of genocide and murder and kidnaping and theft and deception. No one can judge what I have done now, and I can live with it or die with it as I please. It is my decision to choose between disorders.

And so I am content tonight, perhaps happier than I have been in my life, and when I lie down, I will listen for a long time to another motion of breathing before I slip into my dreams.

October 5

The sun is easing down over the mountains now. Our tent is gently flapping. We are on top of Mount Mitchell, the highest point east of the Rockies. Willie is splitting wood, and his arm muscles seem larger than I had remembered, almost too large for his shirt. He is definitely getting taller.

I have always grunted when chopping wood, but Willie wastes no motion and doesn't make a sound, his elbows in close as his arms come down with the ax. Already the fire is rippling. It is not cold, but it will be cold by morning.

Today, we drove through the Cherokee Indian reservation in the Smokies and we stopped in Cherokee and I bought Willie some cheap trinkets that he wanted. He could not take his eyes off an Indian who was walking down the street. When I stopped the Indian and pointed out that his garb was that of the Plains Indians, and not Cherokees, he shrugged and grinned and said, "You oughta see my tipi." I nodded understandingly and turned away. He is no more a part of his past than I am a part of the bloody field of Shiloh. Chasing hunger doesn't change with the season or the years or the romance and salvation of the noble savage.

Willie and I talked some about the Indian, but he was far more interested in buying a Japanese hatchet and so forth than in hearing of the terror of the Trail of Tears. I talked with several of the Indians in town while Willie was spending the twenty dollars I gave him, and I was impressed greatly by their good humor, restrained anger, and will to survive despite the worst of conditions.

As we drove further up in the mountains, my ears began to act up terribly and I kept making funny movements with my mouth trying to get my ears to pop. For some reason, Willie thought it was hilarious and I thought he would never stop laughing at me.

Willie has finished chopping. Getting cold.

October 6

We are back in Branton, in time for a short lesson. It was bitterly cold this morning, and neither of us was prepared, our clothes too light. While we struck camp, Willie kept shivering and clapping his hands and saying, "Godalmighty."

Not nearly so cold here, warm in fact. I went out today and bought a heater for Willie's room. He has kept it very neat.

The only problem I have with him is that he resents having to keep his head down when we drive near town. But he understands the problem and has complained only a little.

Now, he is out running in the woods with Africa.

From the house, I cannot see them.

October 7

Charles suddenly appeared this morning, and I crammed Willie into his room and slammed the door shut just before Charles knocked on the front door. Even though it was cool, I did not invite him in and we sat on the front porch.

"So, how are you doing?" he asked.

"Okay. How are you?"

"Don't be coy, Andrew."

"About what?"

"How's your health?"

"Never felt better in my life." That was a small lie. But I do feel rather well.

"I don't understand how that could be, from what I heard."

"Well, I just decided they were wrong."

"They must have been."

"It's all a matter of whether you want to live or not. I've seen people not as sick as me just curl up and croak because they were bored."

"So you're staying busy?"

"You bet. I'll never stop until I have to."

He visibly relaxed and we talked for a while about the World Series and which teams will be in it. He is for the Dodgers, but I hate them and hope they lose.

When Willie came out, he was pale and shaken, and I tried to talk to him, but he ran down to the pond and sat there for a long time. It is good that I live so far out in the country, elsewise this urge to share would be impractical at best.

October 8

Anna called me from Hyannis this morning to tell me her grandson Andrew (named after me) will be getting married in December.

"She's a real nice girl, Andy," she said. She talks too fast when she is excited and I had a hard time understanding her.

"What's her name?" I asked.

"Karen," she said. "She's a real nice girl. She's Jewish."

"No kidding," I said, lighting my pipe.

"I knew you were going to react that way, but really, you'd love her Andy because she is just so sweet and Andrew loves her so much they must make a darling couple."

"React like what?"

"Oh, you know."

"I don't know. I don't care if she's Jewish. What business is that of mine?"

"Oh, it's not that, Andy."

"Then what?"

"Oh, just don't worry. But can you come to the wedding? You know how much Andrew likes you and it would be so nice to see you again. Paul says he'd love to sit down and talk with you."

"Where will it be and when?"

"December thirtieth in a church in Provincetown."

"I'll be there," I promised without thinking.

We talked about family matters for a while and then she told me again what a nice girl Andrew's fiancée is and how they really do—can you believe it—make a darling couple.

October 9

I met Callie at her place for lunch today. Instead of a servant bringing in food on a tray, we ate in the kitchen where she made us bacon-and-egg sandwiches. I noticed that as she prepared the food, her hands were shaking slightly, as if the whole house were trembling from a passing train's rumble.

After we ate, we took a long walk in a steady drizzle and I felt very strong when she talked to me. And then something went all wrong. I don't know how it happened, but I told her about Willie. She was startled and then surprised and then horrified, I thought, before she became pensive for a while.

"You must care for him quite a lot," she said.

"I must," I said, bewildered.

The rain got harder, and before we got home, her hair was hanging down beside her face and her make-up had become smeared.

October 10

The wildflowers are still high, most of them. My yard is yellow with camphor weed. But the Queen Anne's lace has died, and before long, each wildflower I see will curl into its winter breathing and rest down there underground beyond sleep.

The mornings are cool now and we have entered a season away from the breathless heat of summer. This was the hottest, driest summer I ever remember. But then memory is selective, and forgetting the tides and seasons is much easier than forgetting a certain unkind word or the way a young girl's hair shone in lamplight.

I have been startled that Willie has continued his studies and has become more curious than ever about things. Lately, in the evenings I have taken to playing classical music for him and he seems really to enjoy it. His favorite has been the overture to *Fra Diavolo* by Daniel Auber, a spirited march in the military manner. Also, he enjoys Beethoven, but he professes not to like Mozart that much and he positively cannot abide baroque music. Next to the overture, his favorite music has been Wagner.

I have tried to analyze this, and I have discovered that I do not know how music moves people or what he hears or if it is the same thing I hear.

October 11

A pleasant, sunny Saturday, warm even. I was awakened this morning by the calling of crows down the hill near the pond. They were shrieking and cajoling at each other, their voices tumbling in counterpoint, and for a moment I thought I could hear the voices of a fugue in the stillness.

I decided first thing that it would be a fine day to go fishing, so I told Willie we would drive down to Lake Oconee, a new lake made when the power company dammed up the river. There, in a cove I know, we would be safe from prying eyes. Willie was delighted.

I told him to make us some bologna sandwiches while I got the fishing gear together, but he was puzzled by procedural problems: when does the mustard go on? The bologna? The lettuce? Do you put mustard on the bologna or on the bread? And so on.

The day rose marvelously. We made the cove. No one saw us all day. The fish were striking constantly. Once, I hooked some kind of monster that snapped my line. A carp, I suppose, because another time I hooked a ten-pound carp. We let it go and Willie always laughs at carp because they are so ugly.

He caught a six-pound bass, the largest he'd ever snagged. I promised him I would have it mounted so we froze it. On the way home, I bought a six-pack of beer and as we scaled and gutted out the catch this evening, we both drank. Willie never betrayed any sort of intoxication, but sometimes he would laugh a little too loud.

October 12

I tried reading this morning from the Book of Daniel. Willie had gone for the day, slipping away early, leaving me a short note. But when I sat down with the Bible, I could not concentrate because I am suffocated with Puritan thoughts of sin and the devil and hell and the eternal goodness of many people I know who have no religion.

An old man should be certain at least of these things. But I have steered out of the harbor again in search of that order I have sought for my life. Each new island has that promise before it is raked into the sea by disbelief, pride, or anger. And so it is now, trying to regain something of my childhood from religion, the warmth and security I felt.

And I think of the Indians and how the Dakota believed that God lived in the Black Hills, and spoke to them. Why is their vision of God less than ours? Why is it not the true vision and ours but a legend selected for redemption by literate scholars over the centuries?

I have no idea. I closed my Bible today after trying to read it. Then I read some Tennyson. I took some comfort from it.

October 13

It is midnight, almost the next day. Willie is asleep in his room. The heater works very well, and he stays warm all night.

I went to visit Callie tonight. She met me at the door, looking fragile, perhaps almost frail, and her eyes seemed to take up half her face.

She led me into the den and we sat together on the couch.

"I need for you to kiss me," she said, looking down.

I took her face in my hands and we kissed. Her face felt like hide that had been in the sun too long. She was wearing no make-up. She put her arms around me and pulled herself close. We kissed some more.

"You don't know how lonely it is in this house," she said, her head still against my shoulder.

"I know how lonely it is in my house," I said.

"But it is killing me. I miss you holding me, Andrew. I miss being next to you."

"I never wanted us to be apart."

"I know that. I was just afraid. I was afraid my husband would be angry, rest his soul. We were together so long."

"I don't think he would mind your being happy," I said.

She nodded but she could not speak anymore. Then when she regained her composure we talked for about an hour, before she took me to the bedroom. I had a lot of trouble but she helped me and it was all right.

Shadows are chasing both of us.

October 14

Today is the anniversary of the Battle of Hastings, so I told Willie the story but he seemed confused about the sides, trying to understand them in terms of France and England. I told him it was in the year 1066 and he wanted to know if that was before Columbus.

"Several hundred years," I said.

"Then nobody here knew that battle happened," he said.

"No, not until hundreds of years later."

137

"That's crazy, something happened somewhere and nobody knowing about it."

October 15

I invited Callie out for lunch today. Ahead of time, I told Willie that she would be coming and that he didn't have to hide and he seemed very pleased by that, although if I hadn't ordered him to stay, he likely would have left.

The lunch went very well. We ate fish and hushpuppies. I made Willie cook the fish and he did it perfectly.

Callie told me, aside, that she had no idea what kind of boy Willie was. She pictured him as some wild urchin. I had made Willie dress in a new turtleneck sweater and blue slacks. She was greatly impressed.

I was thrilled. Vanity, all is vanity, saith the preacher.

After lunch, we went for a walk down by the pond and I had thoughts of asking her to marry me, but I could only tell her of the habits of *Castor* and his aquatic cohorts.

October 16

I can't keep this up. He is not my child and she is not my wife. I mucked up the whole lot.

October 17

Depressed. Bitter. Lonely. Vulnerable. Bored.

October 18

Feeling better today. Perhaps I am getting arteriosclerosis. Some days the thoughts seem too far away to grasp. While I was brooding in front of the fire last night, Willie brought me a cup of coffee he'd made himself.

It was very hard to keep from crying about that. It cleared some of the cobwebs out. I am not very gracious for all my blessings.

I weighed in the bathroom today and I have gained weight since the doctors told me I was doomed. I laughed out loud and wanted to go horseback riding or take a long hike. We will walk back up to the north end of the pond tomorrow and survey some before the ducks leave.

October 19

My car engine would not turn over this morning, and so I raised the hood to take a look. Willie craned in beside me. I tried to scrape off the connections on the battery cable and then I got back inside and started it. But Willie, whom I could not see, was still leaning down with his hand inside the hood and the fan blade nicked the index finger on his right hand when the engine caught.

He screamed and was holding it down and mashing it and blood was going everywhere. I dragged him inside (literally) and held a towel against it, but it wouldn't stop bleeding.

"I'm gonna bleed to death," he said, pale and trembling.

"We'll go to the hospital," I said.

"Somebody'll see me," he said.

"Maybe not," I said. I felt sick to my stomach. His pants were getting wet and a puddle on the floor made the oak boards slippery. We drove off and I could not believe that any of it was happening. I saw the road as through a veil of water and I could not decide how I felt.

Luckily, the people at the hospital did not know who I was and I had cash to pay for getting his finger sewed up. I told them I was just passing through town when my car broke and my grandson got nicked by the fan blade. The doctor gave Willie some free pills. All the way home, lying down in the back seat, Willie was groaning a little bit.

When we got home, he took a long nap, sleepy, apparently, from the drug. As he slept, I looked at him and he reminded me strongly of pictures of myself at that age. He awoke and his finger pained him terribly and he only stared at me, answering in monosyllables.

We did no surveying today. I feel useful.

October 20

We did not have school today as Willie's hand hurt terribly.

He was taking a nap about 2 P.M. when I saw a young girl down the hills a way from the house, standing perfectly still, like a sculpture, staring at the house. I watched her for a long time. It might have been the girl with whom I had seen Willie. She was small, but with breasts that seemed too large, long, dirty blonde hair and blue jeans. Then her hands came slowly up to her head and she lightly rubbed the back of her neck as if it hurt and she were attempting to salve the pain.

Then I got the feeling she knew I was watching her, though I do not think she could have. She cocked her head like a curious squirrel and took a half step backward and then pivoted and was gone.

I walked onto the back porch but I could see no trace of her.

She did not look afraid, though. And yet there was something else, perhaps a false toughness, and inner vulnerability that spoke to me through the falling leaves.

October 21

Amos Crick died last night. I heard it on the local radio station this morning while I was cooking breakfast. It was a cold, almost clinical announcement, saying he had died suddenly at his home. I called the house and talked to his widow, who didn't seem all that choked up about it.

"He was watchin' a rerun of 'Hee Haw' and stood up to unloosen his belt and just slud down on to the floor," she said. "Dangest thing I ever saw. I asked what was awrong but he just laid there, so I went over to him and he was sort of bluish and I figured he was mighty sick so I called the doctor and told him about it and he said he was likely dead already. He was."

Her voice didn't sound like somebody in shock. She

seemed a little sad, but it was more as if she had been inconvenienced. I thought back over the years I had known Amos and concluded that I would not really miss him, that he was a crude and thoughtless man. But somehow, as Donne says, his death diminishes me.

Willie is feeling much better despite his hurt hand, and he spent the afternoon after lessons shooting his BB gun.

October 22

Amos Crick's funeral today was as odd as any I've ever seen. He had only a brother and Mrs. Crick must have no family at all. I was at the cemetery and there were only about ten people there. Mrs. Crick was wearing a sort of orange windbreaker that said "Property of the New York Jets," as well as pedal pushers.

While the minister was reading from Ecclesiastes, the Mrs. was trying like hell to light a cigarette in the wind. When she got it lit, she walked over and patted the coffin like you pat a dog on the head to make it go away, tentative, without much affection.

Then she turned away and started walking off before the preacher finished, and this totally unnerved the preacher who just stopped reading and kept gulping until he shrugged and turned to the funeral director and said, sotto voce, "He's all yours."

I hung around and threw a clod of dirt on his coffin. I looked at the little plaque the funeral home had set up and read that Amos was born on October 20, 1906. He died on his birthday.

Later, I stopped by the house to pay my condolences, and I found Mrs. Crick making a pot roast while watching the

"Newlywed Game" on a small black-and-white TV in her kitchen.

October 23

Louis Percy dropped by today, and I scarcely recognized him since he has lost (as he told me) seventy pounds since early summer. He said that shortly after he saw me he had one of those intestinal bypass operations.

"Well, I guess you feel a lot better now that you've lost all that weight," I suggested.

"Actually, I've gotten real nervous and can't stop losing weight," he said with a self-conscious laugh.

"Oh, surely you can eat enough to keep your weight up."

"No, I can't. I think I made a big mistake."

"You couldn't have done it by dieting?"

"I was impatient. I couldn't wait. It was too much work."

"Well, I understand that."

"But I was terribly wrong not to have patience. I'm paying for it now."

We talked for an hour and he never referred to it again, but it clung to him like a ghost or a second skin as we spoke.

October 24

Willie's hand has sealed against disease, and the soreness is disappearing, but slowly. Our schooling has faltered somewhat because I am paying too much attention to history and English and not enough to other subjects.

Late this morning, after we had discussed the Minnesota Sioux Wars of 1862, I read him Poe's story "The Tell-Tale Heart," without thinking of its effect on him. It was a terrible error in judgment, and halfway through I tried gracefully to quit but he wouldn't let me. When I had finished, with the beating of the hidden heart still moving through my words, he sat grimly on the edge of his chair and I felt my palms grow wet.

His eyes seemed glazed and he stared at a spot on the wall, saying nothing for a long time. Then I interrupted his intense reverie and read "Annabel Lee," which turned him more melancholy than ever, but his anger seemed to fade.

"He musta loved her," Willie said.

"I guess so," I nodded. He went outside after that and walked by himself for a long time against the cool day, around the edge of Shadow Pond. His footsteps beat softly against the deep, marshy grass.

October 25

Have I committed some terrible act? It haunts me these lingering days as if I had harmed a child or a woman or taken something of value from someone I loved.

My memory is like a half-seen pond of ice. In my tunnel vision, characters, images skate from one side to the other, half-glimpsed in twilight, filled with familiar curves and angles, almost becoming some word I can whisper into the darkness. But the vapor that rises from the ice is the price of having lived longer than memory will allow, longer than some cherished moment now forgotten as the wind forgets the pattern it plowed through the grain.

Sometimes I feel as if I can harm no one, that even my breathing is benevolent. And then I feel this darkness rising within me, scattering my treasured moments like horses before a storm.

October 26

I will ask Callie to marry me. We will move away and raise Willie as our own. He will grow strong and I will live longer than anyone expected because I cannot die with this life in my keeping.

Or else I will do nothing of the sort.

The dictatorship of the classroom leaves one unprepared for the solitude of retirement. Making decisions was a lovely part of bringing ideas to life, telling students when they would study, when they would write, when they would be tested. You have the right to rule them as if your bloodline were royal and their fathers had given you their sincerest vote.

Willie, of course, is not here. I worry about him catching cold. Can I nurse him, I who never before nursed anyone? Sara always refused my fumbling caresses when she was ill and she took care of me then as if I were a fragile child, frail from some childhood malady. So how could I succor Willie if he should fall ill?

I must not brood upon such things.

The air is fresh and bright. Fall is upon my old house and my bones drift with the delicious melancholy that always comes when frost comes and death comes and school comes back again.

October 27

When I saw Bill coming, I told Willie to go down into his room, but he just sat there and stared at me. I began to panic and begged for the good of both of us to go down. He would not move.

Bill came to the door. I was going to tell him to go away, that I was sick with a contagious disease, but I could only croak a feeble hello as he passed me going inside. Willie remained bolted to the chair in the living room.

BILL: Oh, hello. You visiting Dr. Lachlan?

ANDREW: *(Excitedly.)* He's my nephew just down for a few days. His name is Harold Olsen. He's from Buffalo. Say hello, Harold.

WILLIE: *(With a malicious grin.)* Hello. What's your name? *(Lord, that accent. No way he's from Buffalo.)*

BILL: I'm Bill McAdam. So.

ANDREW: *(Wringing his hands.)* Sit down, Bill. Didn't I hear you caught three touchdown passes Friday night?

BILL: Got lucky, that's what it was. Then Gene, he's the QB *(He said "QB," not quarterback.)* was right on line. It was a piece of cake.

WILLIE: What kind of cake?

BILL: *(Happily.)* Devil's food. That's my favorite. What's yours?

WILLIE: Vaniller.

At this point, I thought Willie was going to burst out laughing, and I could tell Bill was quite confused. I was almost shaking.

BILL: You look kind of familiar. Have I seen you before?
WILLIE: One summer I give tours at the Statue of Liberty. Maybe you seen me there.
BILL: *(Puzzled.)* No, I've never been there before.
WILLIE: You ought to visit it sometime. It's enchanting.

Enchanting? Where did he get that? By this time, I was trying hard not to laugh. I stood and told Bill we were just planning to leave, and that he should come back sometime. He said he would do that, he would come back.

WILLIE: Our pleasure to meet you.
BILL: How long you staying?
WILLIE: *(With sickening sweetness.)* I leave that up to my uncle.

October 28

Willie has been reading the papers as an assignment and has decided he is strongly for a larger army. I asked him why.

"We need one of them," he said.

"Why do you want a strong army?" I asked.

"To smack some heads." He said it like I was crazy to have asked. I am going to try to question him some about his home life when he was younger, because, despite his enthusiasm, there is a darkness that lingers around him something like an echo.

October 29

I gave Willie a test today on the Sand Creek Massacre. The questions, I thought, were relatively simple, basic inquiries into the motives of Colonel Chivington and his Colorado "100-day soldiers."

I had expected rambling answers, but I was unprepared for the almost incoherent results I got. I looked at his paper and he watched me as I looked at it, an almost predatory glare in his eyes.

"Willie, this is a mess," I said sadly.

"I told you I ain't that good at learning," he said, staring at me with cold, hard eyes.

"But my God, you've got a good mind, son. Why haven't you listened better than this?"

"I listen," he said stubbornly. "Sometimes I don't hear."

"Well, you better get on the stick," I seethed.

"What are you going to do?" he asked. "Hold me back a year? Send a note home to my pa? Call the cops?"

I could feel the color flood into my cheeks as I stood and grabbed him and flung him across my lap. He struggled furiously and raised his arm to strike but could not do it. I slammed my palm across his rear four or five times. The strength and the anger suddenly dissolved. I felt like I could not move.

Willie jumped up. He was shaking slightly, like he would cry. He pointed his finger at me like God.

"Don't you never lay another hand on me you god-damned old son of a bitch!" he shouted. Then he turned and bolted through the door, gone down the hill before the screen door had finished slamming behind him.

Now it is late and I do not know if he will ever return. I sat with my head in my hands for a long while, listening to

Chopin nocturnes. But my head swam and no thoughts would be completed before another came.

If I could, I would take his head in my hands and kiss it and tell him that no history can console us for our own past and no sonnet can salve cruel words from someone you love.

October 30

Rain is streaking my windows. It is cool, a slight wind coming in from the east. They say it will get colder later today. I built a fine fire this morning and ate sausage and eggs and drank strong black coffee, a blend (is that right?) from Tanzania or somewhere in Africa, very high in caffeine, bracing. After eating, I catalogued nineteen books, pausing to flip casually through an old copy of *Lust for Life* by Irving Stone, a fine book and one I remember well from many years ago. Then I read a short time from some other things and . . .

Oh, God. Where is he?

November 1

When I awoke this morning, Willie was standing over my bed. His arms were folded across his chest and something was in his hand. He thrust out his fist and it was paper and I took it and sat up in bed and reached for my glasses and found them and turned on the light. Here is what it said:

> Col. Chiventen was a man who hated Indian. He hated them like whits hated black folks here. He took his armie to where some Shyanes was camped near a fort where they had told to go. Then he let loose his men and they killed and mutalited the Indian women and children. It was massacur, one of worse in history. The Shyanes and then the Seoiux got together and begun to kill whits. And they had it coming. Then war come to the plains.

It was written in pencil and the handwriting was studied and cramped, and erasures were evident in several places. He rewrote "Sioux" several times before settling on his spelling. The paper was nearly worn through from erasures and in places looked like a fine piece of lace.

I got up, naked from my bed and walked into the kitchen. Willie was sitting at the table eating a peanut butter sandwich and drinking a tall glass of milk.

"Is that right?" he asked.

"It's perfect," I said. "I'm sorry I hit you, Willie. That was stupid."

" 's all right," he said quickly. "I acted up stupid."

I suddenly realized I was naked and felt ashamed and tried to cover myself, but Willie acted as if I were fully clothed and I edged out of the room, feeling as if I had done something terribly foolish.

We resumed classes this morning, even though it was Saturday. He wanted to know something about the War Between the States, so I told him some of the story of the Battle of Shiloh. After that, we talked about *Gone With the Wind.* Willie saw it on TV and he said it made him sad and that he didn't understand it all.

November 2

I overslept this morning and when I dressed and went into the kitchen, I was startled to see Willie sitting alongside the girl I had seen at the foot of the hill that slopes down to Shadow Pond. I felt my skin tighten as if it would burst and I scarcely knew what to say. She was wearing a nice windbreaker and now close I could tell she was, in fact, quite pretty, with light blue eyes, almost transparent. She looked at Willie and then back at me, gulping.

"Well, good morning," I mumbled. "Willie, who's your friend?" Willie walked behind her and put his hands on her shoulders.

"This here's Carleen. Carleen, this here's Dr. Lackland."

"Carleen," I nodded. "You live around here?"

"Down there," she said in a fragile voice, pointing southwest.

"Where down there?" I asked.

"Out on Amberjack Road," she almost whispered. I thought. God, that was four miles away at least.

"Then you are Willie's friend?"

"I'm his girl," she said, and she blushed deeply and looked down.

"I'm going to marry her," Willie announced.

"You're what?"

"Not now," he said. "Someday, though." He looked at me like *cool it*. I did. I cooked breakfast for them and I could tell by her voice that she was not from around here originally and she said she had moved here with her family from Indiana two years ago. She talked in a quick, clipped voice.

Was she the girl with whom I saw Willie in bed? I could not tell, but I could not get it out of my mind. Later, after we ate, they left to go for a walk and when Willie came back late in the afternoon, she was not with him anymore.

November 3

I had lunch today with Robert Butler, an old friend who is retired from the building supply business. I had not talked to him in several years until he called last night and invited me out.

Robert is a massive man, with a head that is bald and domed, and flat, thick features and stiff bristles of hair growing out of his nose. When he talks, the words seem to come out of his nose rather than his mouth, and he has some nervous facial tics that are fascinating to watch.

We talked about very little of substance, except to relive some of the days when we were at the University of Georgia together, now more than fifty years ago. Somehow, I felt sorry for him because I heard his wife, an invalid in a nursing home, lost her mind.

No more horrible future than that, I decided.

November 4

I sense a change in Willie, as if somehow he is no longer unwise to the peril of our situation or of his future, and how I have manipulated it. He does not seem sullen, but often I see his face fallen as if something were troubling him in an almost abstract way, the look a philosopher gets when he comes to doubt a theory he had held dear.

He studies, he listens, he tries to accomplish something that will make me proud. But something desperate is coming up like a fish surfacing, and I cannot stop him and I cannot tell him what it is.

November 5

I awoke early this morning and went to awaken Willie to find that he had gone and everything in his room of value to him, his possessions, had been cleaned out. I stood in a daze in his room looking back up the ladder, feeling dizzy. On the kitchen table, I found this note:

Dear Mister Lackland, I cannot stay here no more. I now that. I have gone home to my mother and live with her. Thank you for keeping care of me as you did. Willie.

I sat at the table in the kitchen. Light was streaming through the window and I could tell it would be a fine day. I made some coffee and sat and sipped. Then I read the morning paper. Then I washed dishes.

Then I sat in the living room and listened to Chopin. Cried some.

November 6

I feel as if I have been morally compromised. I know that he is gone forever from my life, and it leaves a hollow feeling in my stomach, as if I had lost my child again.

I feel terribly alone. I found the syllabus I had made for Willie and I shredded it and burned it in the fireplace. Then I nailed the floor shut to his room.

I wanted to call Callie, but instead I lay on my bed as it began to rain outside and listened to the crying of crows against the low clouds.

November 10

There is nothing to do but keep at it. I must find order. Order is what I am looking for.

November 11

Slowly, slowly, I am awakening.

November 12

I feel as if I have come through fire, purified, a little afraid still, humble.

November 13

I met Callie today, a cold day, cloudy, an east wind puffing up. We sat in her living room and drank tea from Wedgwood china. She knew of my anguish and we did not speak of it. We spoke of our future, and I felt strong as we talked.

"We don't have time," I said, sipping the bitter tea, "to make any plans. I can't think we could ever survive together. We have lived alone for too long."

"I know, Andrew," she nodded. "I've been thinking about it a lot. I can't make our lives more miserable by pretending that our affection could ever lead to something that would make us want to live together."

"We are too different."

"Yes."

"There is happiness in living alone."

"Yes."

"And even though we have love, that is only half enough."

"Yes."

November 14

I feel the strength coming through me like spring. I have always been vain about my recuperative powers. Sometimes I feel as arrogant and strong as Peter the Great, as intelligent as Sitting Bull.

It is good to clean out the details of life sometimes, to break up all the hindrances and pain and retreat to where you were at some earlier, happier time.

That is a great skill, one I think I can master before I die.

November 15

Willie called me today.

"How is your mother?" I asked.

"She's right good to me now," he said. "I been cutting wood, stuff like that. She cooks better than you do." He laughed a little.

"You'll come to see me?" I asked.

"Sure," he said.

Will he come back? I don't think so. I do not think his life will be short of troubles because he has seen the thrill of delight in someone's death earlier than most.

I went out today and bought a new heavy coat and socks. They are attractive.

November 16

Savannah. I drove back down here today and checked in at the same motel as earlier this summer. The weather is cold and windy and it is fine to walk the beach with a cup of steaming coffee.

I love the edge of the land, the eyelid of water blinking over the wrack of shells and seaweed through the night, higher, then back again. There is peace in watching the waves throb and then release. I sat at sunset today, the warmth over my shoulders, and saw seagulls buoyed by the breeze, hovering over the water, waiting. And so I sat in the cold sand, waiting, too, listening for my pulse among the motions of the sea.

It is almost winter now, and my shadow is spreading each day. I live among the waves and shadows, carelessly whispering to my life.

November 17

I have lost my right to scholarship. I do not remember the precise method of making footnotes or the function of transition paragraphs. But then I have been a minor figure always, writing minor articles while teaching at a junior college. They look down their noses at that. "Oh, a *junior college*," as if what you could learn there is so much less than what an educated person would tolerate.

I am thinking of all those bastards today. They can go to hell.

I sneaked Africa into the room with me, and he sprawls across the end of the bed in canine luxury, sometimes running in his sleep as if there is a wildness and freedom left in this world.

I spent much of this morning asking after Janet and I found that she does still work around here sometimes. I passed the word that I'd like to see her. I hope she shows up. I may not have the hands of a shrimper, but my mind is clear and there is a feather edge to what is left of my love.

November 18

Still here. I sat in the sand dunes this morning, looking at myself from above, trying to visualize this movie in which I see myself. And I saw a silent old man with yellow-white hair combing his memories as the cold sun rose, thinking of his wife and the time they went to the beach and scraped shellfish from the bays with long-tined rakes and how the shellfish tasted, raw and dipped in butter sauce. And he remembered her eyes, how they were so blue they became sky during certain benevolent seasons and how her arms came around his always, even until she was so crumpled and arthritic that she could barely move from the sunny chair to the door when he came home.

And he sat in the sand and listened to the thick breathing of his dog as it came galloping up the beach from licking the ball of sun as it washed up out of the sea. And he looked back again into the sun and saw his wife wide-eyed in London, standing near their special park, pointing and laughing, saying over and over, "I can't believe we're here. I can't believe we're here."

And then he put his wife away, back into the comfort of her shroud and felt his face, and it was warm and he was yet alive and he would walk and try to live with as much grace as time gave him.

November 19

Janet showed up at my room late this morning. She stood in a light drizzle, wrapped in a thin coat, looking beautiful and fresh, her face reddened from the wind. I let her in and she sat on the bed for a few minutes.

"Why did you come back?" she asked.

"I wanted a friend," I said with irony and guile.

"After what I did?"

"If you had asked, I would have given you some money. I didn't know you were hard up."

"I wasn't hard up," she sighed. "I just like to steal. I guess it's a character flaw."

"But don't you have a good job? You said you waited tables. Still do that?"

"Sure. I'm okay. You know."

"Just ask."

"It's not the same thing. I always thought I should get things because of who I was, not what I did. And when I didn't get them, I started taking them, and it was all right because I thought they were sort of owed me."

"You still hooking?"

"I'm not here for the rent check."

"It must be a bad life."

"Not as bad as working in a factory. If I'm lucky, somebody treats me with a little tenderness. There's no question of love. But being nice sometimes is enough."

I could not make love, but I paid her anyway and when she left, she put her head on my shoulder for a long time and I could feel her heart beating.

November 20

I am back home. The sky is royally blue and I sit here now in the warmth of midday, under a breath of cedar and Virginia pine, watching the beaver humping in the lake. Fall is the dry season here. But it is a lovely lack of moisture, not like the drought of the breathless summer. This dry time is cool and it makes your skin snap when you walk into it from your house.

Bill McAdam came out for a few minutes this morning on his way to school. He no longer acts so naïve, and he looks at me with more understanding and less pity than before.

He wants to come out on Saturday and go fishing in the pond, and I said sure, I will go with you.

Late autumn is a restorative. Even though death is around, the leaves turning brown and collapsing and then drifting down, you are alive, and there is nothing else to know.

I have drifted this far, across the pages of a vagrant history, through several lives of varied interest, and I shall live more before I whisper colloquies into the eye of darkness.

November 22

He came back today to visit. I felt vulnerable and silly, and I couldn't stop feeling this spreading sadness. His hair has been cropped down to his skull again and he has lost weight. But there is something winning about him again, indigenous and genuine.

"So, are you happy?" I asked. I have never asked him such a question before.

"Getting by. You?"

"Still alive." He smiled, and his teeth were not as clean and I said nothing.

"Your ma all right?"

"She's sick some. Don't hardly seem right in the head some days."

"Ever see your pa's grave?"

"No."

"Like me to take you?"

"I don't think so. Sometime. Later."

We made some cornbread and then he left, and then Bill came over and we went fishing in the pond and talked about football and fall and bluegills and how history repeats itself, though not in that order.

November 23

The sky seems empty today, half cloudy and warm, but with no character or threat of sunfall or rain. I sit here by the pond, Africa asleep in the warm reeds where the water cannot reach. I sip my coffee and listen to the world around me for signs that my stupidity is treated charitably by nature.

Nature, it seems now, is charity itself. I am buoyed by the cattails and the way they pop when you pick their erect thickness. And I am praised by the inner folds of fallen leaves. We are dying together and yet I lack their purpose.

I have worked my life and left few trails, and yet now I feel at peace, purposeful, as if some shade of fame would take me alone and spread the vowels of my name across the water.

November 24

My God, it has happened all over again. They found Willie's mother dead last night, and she was still tightly clutching the .22 pistol she used to shoot herself in the head. I heard it on the radio. I am afraid to go by there. I worry about Willie.

I am sitting here like a coward. It is midmorning. I feel like I am going blind. I feel choked. Was it illness that drove her to this?

How can a child accept both parents dead in such short order? Was there something evil in Willie that hastened their deaths? Did he wish it? Is this his great evil curse to bear and forget for his life?

Poor child. How can I tell you to survive? How can I tell you survival is all there really is?

November 25

I cannot awaken from this dark dream. Callie called me today and told me she was *so* sorry and wanted to know if there was anything she could do. I said something foolish because I hurt so badly. She got huffy and said she was just trying to help and I told her to grow up and quit acting like a child. She hung up. To hell with her.

I am going to bed. Maybe today is it for me. I don't feel well.

November 26

The sky is a high blue and the maples have turned to flame. I feel restored. God is my strength. I went to visit Willie today. He was sitting in his bedroom with his hands in his lap. He looked pale, drawn, and his eyes were popping from their sockets. And yet he was calm. Relatives are there until they decide what to do with him.

"You okay, Willie?" I asked.

"I'm scared," he whispered, in a voice as dry as attic dust.

"Scared of what?"

"Of what I done."

"What have you done?"

"I done let her do this. I couldn't make her understand nothing. She was sick."

"Understand what?"

"I don't know." His eyes were glazed, helpless.

166

His uncle from Monroe is now his legal guardian and I have heard he is not looking to keep Willie up there.

When I came home, I felt sad, but perhaps purified, as if from a refiner's fire. I have been released finally from my search for order in this life.

Now I know that there is order and that in that order I am an unmoving atom on a speck of dust lost among the stars.

November 27

Thanksgiving. Enter His gates with thanksgiving and his courts with praise. Give thanks to Him; bless his name. For the Lord is good. His lovingkindness is everlasting and his faithfulness to all generations.

So much has changed since early summer. I try to accept everything, how I have become lost among my priorities and how I bless and curse my days.

But there is a blessing in the air today, something telling me that outside in the trees and down along Shadow Pond there is more I should learn before I am gone to dust.

And I will spread out past the pond to new friends in the next few months. I must not feel at my death that I have wasted even a minute of this time.

And so today I give thanks that I am still alive enough to feel something real, something past history and the classroom and beyond the strategy of ancient battles.

November 28

When Bill visited today, I felt something for him that I had not before. I do not know what. Perhaps an affection for his care. I'm not sure. He has lately taken to writing poetry, not very good, and he shyly showed some of it to me today and I praised it.

November 29

I thought about the war all day today and got out my book of photos. I could not help looking for the one picture that has stayed with me these years: a dead German soldier who had climbed a tree and was killed there, and when he fell, he was grasped by the limbs. His eyes open, mouth open.

I have never joined the VFW or the American Legion. I feel compassion and love for my fellows there in Europe. I wish now I could see Sal Mitrillio or Buddy Owens. But I do not think life is worth living with war. For those who died, their lot was easier than for those of us who came home.

I walked downtown today and saw many people whom I know. Everyone remarked about how well I look. They are afraid. I wish one would come up to me and say, ''Well, Andrew, you look pretty bad and I think you'll be a stiff by Christmas.''

But they mean well. They are afraid of what I once also feared. The only thing I fear now is time, and that I may not be able to decide, finally, how to use it.

November 30

It snowed today, but only enough to powder the earth. After the snow came, a flock of crows settled in my front yard, hammering at the hard earth for food. I watched them for a long while, until they all seemed to move in a regular rhythm, cocking their heads and spearing me with their dark eyes until I felt they called me to come with them, to follow them to where there is more light and sun among the boughs.

December 1

I hear Willie is in the custody of his uncle in Monroe. I have a blinding compulsion to go up there and talk to him. What would I say? Could I talk to his uncle reasonably and bring Willie home? Do I need professional counseling?

I am going damnit. I want to go get my boy. I want to hold him to me and tell him that dreams are the work of clouds, and that in my walls, he will find love.

I am going up there.

December 2

Called his uncle, Virlyn Threlkeld in Monroe. He sounded like an old man. I told him about Willie staying with me and he listened, interjecting "I be dog" and "I'll swanee" sometimes.

"Well, I do have to say I ain't hardly equipped to have a boy here," he said. I could hear him scratching his face (head?). "Lila's done gone sickly and I'm getting right old and feeble. You'd like to have him down there?"

I told him it would be only temporary, until better arrangements could be made. Lying. Well, he would think about that, about me being his legal guardian.

"Can I come up and talk to you and Willie?" I asked hopefully.

"Sure you can," he said. "How about this evening?"

I am leaving in a few minutes to drive over there. But I will be back late so I am writing now.

December 4

Very cordial meeting with Virlyn and Lila. They talked to me for a long time and said, finally, that they just weren't sure about it all. Willie was with them, but he said little and gave no indication that he was desperate to come back and live with me.

As I left, Willie followed me to the car.

"Do you miss them?" I asked.

"They was mostly mean and ugly folks," he said, expressionless, his lips barely moving.

"Where were you when she did it?"

"Down at the shack with Carleen." I could not bring myself to ask him much more.

"Did you see your ma dead there in the house?"

"When I got back, they was cops all over. A lady with the Jehovah's Witnesses found her. I just stood there staring. It was like it weren't real. I couldn't feel nothing."

I felt a little ill.

"Would you like to come live with me?"

"Why would you be wanting me?" I thought of all the unspoken words from my life, of the times I had never said things I felt.

"Because I love you like a son," I said. He nodded and put his hand gently on my arm and then was gone into the house. I was trembling. Despite the cold east wind, I was sweating, too.

174

December 5

I made application in the courts for legal guardianship of Willie. It will be several days, perhaps weeks before anything is decided. Until then, Willie will live with Virlyn and Lila in Monroe.

So now it comes to waiting.

I will try to stay busy. Today, I read a book called *Lame Deer, Seeker of Visions,* by a Sioux Indian of that name. After I finished it, the sky was nearly dark, but as usual I felt close to the earth so I walked through the drizzle down to Shadow Pond and put out in the boat as the sun was settling down. Behind the clouds, the sun faded away. I paddled to the eastern side of the pond, feeling my muscles push against the water, listening to it swirl and lap at the boat. My muscles became swollen with blood, and I could almost hear the sound of water talking to me, telling me in its native tongue that I, too, am water and that nothing hard can last before the water or the wind.

Then came the bird calls, and I tried to listen to them for voices, for the start of a vision of the real world, not the globe of ideas or speculation. But I could only hear their dark vowels in the wind.

What a fit father, I mulled, who drifts under a cold drizzle, listening for messages from the rush of dark wings.

December 6

Callie called.

She said how wonderful it was about Willie and that she heard I was trying to get custody. Yes, I said, it is wonderful and I am doing that. Well, she said, why don't we get together and talk about it, and I said, no, I don't think there would be any good in that. And she said, I understand, but I don't think she did.

Louis Percy called today and said he was bringing some students down from the University on Tuesday, if that was all right, to meet me here on my own turf and talk about history. I almost shouted yes into the phone. Yahoo! It's going to be a good month!

December 7

I cannot write this date without remembering. I had only been at Mt. Russell for a few years then. Sara was strong and beautiful. We were listening to a record of Beethoven's Seventh Symphony when Dean Chase called to say turn on the radio, the Japs have bombed Pearl Harbor. I didn't know where Pearl Harbor was, and Sara thought it was in California, so when we found out it was Hawaii, we were a little relieved instead of being more horrified.

It was a cold day. We had the grate full of coal and it was glowing red. We sat side-by-side on the couch and held hands as the news reports came in. School classes were canceled. The next day we sat in the same place and listened to President Roosevelt declare war over the radio.

Those years that passed since then have been ripped like leaves from a calendar. Sicily, Italy, Austria, and then back home. And then all those years as we turned gray and reminisced.

And so few today have taken note of what happened. I recall how Mother cried when I enlisted, saying I was too old and this was for younger men. But Sara understood and said she would pray for me every night. Later, she told me she did in fact pray for me every night until I came home.

There was a small notice of it in the paper today, almost apologetic, as if nobody were alive who cared anymore.

December 8

I spent much of today working on a new monograph about the Powder River Expedition of 1865. I have so many articles Xeroxed about it but I was sure there was some angle that had not yet been covered in the process.

Writing history is comforting to me. When I wrote my book about Colonel Henry Carrington, and Fort Phil Kearny, it was about the happiest time of my life. I never hope to regain the pleasure of tracing his life from the east to Ohio and then to the terror of the post-Civil War West when the Sioux were determined to save their hunting grounds.

Perhaps it is the urge to share in the action of the moment, something I have always been constitutionally unsuited to do. I have always been a rather timid man, lingering too long in the darkness, half in love with silence. And yet, when I see, even in my mind, the sweep of men and motives, I somehow know that any small indiscretion of mine will go unnoticed.

That's a comforting thought.

December 9

Louis came down with his students, five of them, looking so young and serious and solemn I wanted to laugh. Louis looks even worse than before, his face nothing but skeleton and skin. He is trying to grow a beard to cover it up, but the beard is thin and patchy and just makes him look like a wandering ascetic.

The students were rather wanting to sit at my feet for knowledge as it were, so to break that up, I cracked a bottle of Evan Williams and we all sat and sipped, even though it was not yet noon.

They had read my book as part of their course and had also read excerpts that Louis had made from two of my other books, one about the Cherokees and the other about the Sand Creek Massacre of the Southern Cheyennes.

One of the students, a young woman with lake-blue eyes, kept asking me rather good questions and I felt an ugly urge to know more about her. Her name was Hannah, and she wore a long dress, the old, muslin kind, and wore a knitted shawl around her shoulders. She seemed without guile or pretense. Her laugh was a little on the raucous side, but she didn't seem to care.

Aside, I asked Louis about her, and he said she was a senior majoring in American history and that she was from Sylva, North Carolina, which is near the Cherokee Indian Reservation.

I asked him if he thought she might have supper with me and he looked at me skeptically, but I winked and it seemed to lift him out of his sunken body, and he promised to call me with her phone number when he got it out of her records.

I paid special attention to her the rest of the time they were there, and I got very drunk as they did. Right now, as I write this, I am still drunk, but rather mellow, now that night has come and anything can come true.

December 10

Bill came over this afternoon and brought his new girlfriend, a syrupy, saccharine, overpainted girl named Hillary Atchison. She was too much for me.

BILL: Hillary's an artist. She makes these beautiful pictures with sand, don't you, Hillary?

HILLARY: Oh, I just kid around, you know? I mean it seems to me that God put us here on this good earth for a purpose and maybe he just meant for me to be an artist, you know?

ANDREW: I know.

HILLARY: I mean, we should all try and fulfill ourselves to the best of our abilities. And gosh, I just found I could do this thing and I guess the Lord is leading me to do it.

BILL: She did a sand painting of Elvis and one of Jesus, too.

ANDREW: Gosh.

HILLARY: Now Billy, you're just boring Mr. Lachlan.

ANDREW: Gosh, I don't think that's boring.

HILLARY: *(With giddy approval.)* Really? Well, you're just being sweet, that's all, just being sweet. Some people think it's just boring but Billy doesn't and makes me tell people about it and I think, well, they're just going to be bored, but then somebody'll come along who's not and it's all worthwhile, you know?

ANDREW: I know.

I like Bill, but his taste in females is appalling. I think he was a little embarrassed.

December 11

Louis called this morning and gave me Hannah's phone number. Her full name is Hannah Elaine Gibbs. I called her this morning, but her roommate was the only one there so I gave her my number and asked her to tell Hannah to call collect.

She called about the middle of the afternoon, her voice full of questions and hesitation. We chatted for a few minutes about history and she told me how much she liked my books and so forth. My hands were getting wet on the phone.

"Look here, would you like to come down and have supper with me?" I blurted.

"I'd love to," she said quickly. I couldn't think of what to say next. I was ready for her to treat me like a grandfather, an officious boor. "Are you still there?"

"Yes," I said, clearing my throat. "I guess we've got trouble on the line." What a lousy liar I am. We set things up for Sunday night. I offered to come get her, but she drives and has her own car and insisted she would come by herself.

Now what?

December 12

I am terribly sick.

December 13

Yesterday I had chills and then sweated and something in my innards went haywire, hurting like somebody sticking a red hot poker in me and twisting it. I suppose this is a sign for me to take, but I only feel anger now. I got out of bed last night and sat in the freezing air on the porch for a long time and I began to feel better.

There was an owl making music then, and it seemed as if it were talking to me, and I tried to listen for its message, but I could find nothing there but consolation and the feeling of having perhaps been a bird in some other life.

I tried to imitate the owl's cry but then it went silent and I knew that whatever I had said was wrong, that to make any sound when an owl speaks to you is wrong. I should have waited and maybe I would have heard its message on the next gust of wind.

When I came back inside, I began to sweat in gallons, and by the time I went to bed, I had soaked right through my clothes. I awoke this morning feeling fine and strong, my head clear.

Perhaps it was some kind of vision from the other world, a few moments to warn me before I learn to fly.

December 14

I am strong, profoundly grateful for whatever has spared me thus far. Hannah will come over tonight, so I am writing this at mid-morning. I took a long walk upon arising today and stumbled upon the carcass of a beaver at the far end of the pond. Its fur and entrails had disappeared and bits of skin only clung to the skeleton, and I looked through the bones to see if I could tell what killed it, but I have no expertise in such post mortems.

As I poked through the bones with a stick, I felt sad that this marvelous beast should die like this. But as I stirred the whitening bones, I felt a little comforted, because it had become part of nature. It had not been sentenced to some steel vault or the eternity of a satin cushion and fine linens.

And so it cheered me, and I did not stir the bones any more. I wish I could leave my bones on some forest trail where the wind and mottled sunlight could pick them clean. That is something to die for.

Talk of death frightens me not at all. But I am not ready just yet. I can feel my bones cracking with new life. I can feel *Castor* rising through my arms, and my fingers becoming webbed down there by the pond where everything is alive. I feel like swimming or singing.

December 15

The evening with Hannah was a tremendous success, though I confess I feel a little lecherous. I cooked spaghetti, using Sara's old recipe, and we drank red wine while we ate. She was again wearing a long dress, almost as if she knew how much I loved seeing it. She did not look at me like an old man, and I think I looked rather distinguished for such an old fool. And God, those eyes.

She washed the dishes and we lit a fire and sat around drinking wine and I acted as witty and urbane as possible, fearing in the back of my mind that pain again. But I never felt better. Her face got flushed from the fire and we talked about ourselves then, very personal things that neither one of us thought we could say.

"I get so lonely sometimes," she said. "I broke up with my boyfriend about six months ago, and I don't miss him, but you miss being around people. I go home sometimes, but family's not the same. Now, I don't know what I'm going to do when I graduate."

"Graduate school?" I suggested.

"Do you ever get lonely?" she asked, ignoring my remark.

"I'm trying to learn to become part of nature," I shrugged. "It hasn't worked too well. I keep listening for messages from willows and water lilies and beavers and fish, but they must not want to talk to me."

"What do you think they would say?"

"Probably nothing," I muttered.

"I think they would say you have earned their trust," she nodded. "I think they would teach you how to listen to them and become part of what they are."

"Why do you think so?"

"I just do," she said. All this was not too familiar, not as cozy or improper as it sounds. But it was very special for me. Finally, she had to go, and we stood at the door and I tried not to look into her eyes.

"I enjoyed this more than you can imagine," I said.

"Me, too," she said meekly. "I never talked to anyone like this before."

"It was fun."

Then she put her firm hands on my shoulders and kissed me lightly on the cheek, and I wanted to kiss her on the mouth but I could not move to do it. But I squeezed her hand then.

What is in her mind? I have found that you are never too old to feel what you felt as a young person, only too bored. When she left, I let the fire die down and then did something I hadn't done in years.

December 16

Virlyn called today and told me that Willie could come live with me.

"This has been real sad for me and the wife, what with my sister and her man both dying like that," he said. "Our health ain't all that good . . ." His voice trailed off.

"I applied for guardianship like we talked about," I said. I felt shaky all over, wondering if he would change his mind.

"Well, I think it's for the best," he said. I never mentioned my health. I was not adopting him, just becoming his guardian.

I called the judge today and if all goes well, she sees no reason why Willie can't be with me before Christmas. That is a happy thought!

Things will be different, but they will still be good for both of us. They have to be.

This afternoon, I unnailed Willie's room and cleaned it up. Already, lichens or something like that had begun to grow down the walls and I felt like I was clearing the dust from a tomb.

There is some fine distinction between fear and love, but I have not lived well enough to define it.

December 17

I imagined today what it would be like for Hannah to call me. But the feeling wore thin quickly and I found myself wandering down the road by my house. All the honeysuckle and blackberry vines are dead now, wizened and sere, knotted in death. But still they snake through the branches of small trees.

I watched a large black ant cross the road. I tried to think of how to describe him, and all I could decide was "succulent." He wandered as if stunned by a blast, stumbling from pebble to pebble, feeling them warily, then heading on, drawn by some strong pheromone.

I walked some more. I felt the red earth hard under my feet. I felt like singing Christmas carols. I sang "O Come, All Ye Faithful," "O Come, O Come, Emmanuel." I could see someone taking me for a beggar or a madman, caparisoned in my mackinaw and singing grandly down the road.

When I began to wear down, I hummed as I turned around and came back up the other side of the road. Even out here, I thought, those you love are never far away. I thought of him.

Later. It is now nearly 10 P.M. and darkness has clamped down over Branton. I have a fire crackling on the hearth and next to me is a small glass of bourbon. A tumbler, actually. (Where did that name come from?)

I am absorbed with one question this evening. I have not been able either to work or get drunk. This is the question: Am I being honest with myself? I scarcely know how to answer that. Am I selfish? Surely, but is that my motivation for living with Willie? When I speak or write, whose words do I use? Some sage historian or forgotten silly poet of romance? Do I use now the words of my students whose theses have become my own ideas? Is there anything left of what I was before I understood the sorrow of the world?

I cannot separate love from desire, hate from envy, or price from cost. The more I ponder on distinctions, the more I wallow in generalities. Is this the way it must be? Am I so shallow that I cannot understand even the heartbeat of the beaver in Shadow Pond?

Yes, I think the answer to that one, Dr. Lachlan, is most definitely yes.

December 18

Virlyn left Willie with me today and Willie looked darkly nervous and unsure of things. Everything has been settled. As Virlyn drove off, Willie stood there with his small, sad suitcase in his hand. After Christmas, Willie will be going back to public school; things will not be the same.

But we talked shortly after he got settled and Willie
wanted to clear one thing up right away.

"You was scared for me?" he asked.

"Yeah," I said.

"I never had nobody scared for me." He said it only with
slight emotion, as if he could not quite believe it.

"I was that."

"What am I supposed to call you? Grandpaw, or Mr.
Lackland, or . . . what, I . . ." His voice faded. I tried to
think of something to say that would put the choice in his
hands. You're supposed to do that these days. No luck.

"I kind of like 'Grandfather,' " I said. He looked at me
suspiciously, as he had done so many times.

"That's funny sounding."

"Then what do you like?" I swore I wasn't going to say
that.

"I'd like to call you what Mr. Percy called you. You told
me what he called you. He called you 'Doc.' I'd just as lief
call you Doc."

"I'd rather you call me grandfather."

"I'll think on it," he said.

I thanked God with all my heart for this blessing in my
life. My son has come home from the shroud.

December 19

I made a big show today. I suppose I was just being vain, but
I took Willie into town and ate with him at the Country Pine
and then took him to the middle drug store for an ice cream.
I explained to Willie they called it the middle drug store because there were at one time three drug stores on the block,

but that one of them had closed and the one that used to be in the middle was now on the end.

"That's awful dumb," quoth Willie.

People came up to me and you could see it in their eyes that they thought it was a good thing I did in taking Willie. If they knew this relationship's history . . .

Later I asked him what he wanted for Christmas.

"I'd kind of like to have one of them race-car sets, Doc," he said gleefully.

"I'd like to have a race car set, *Grandfather*."

He just stared at me stonily. I harrumphed around a little, but secretly I do not mind. We drove out to the mall and I bought him the damndest race-car set you ever saw as sort of a pre-Christmas gift. I don't want to lavish too much on him, but I have more money than I could ever spend.

We brought it home and set it up in front of the fire and then we raced. I was not very good and Willie easily took me for five dollars. I've learned my lesson from that.

December 20

She called me today, Hannah did. She said she wanted me to come with her to a Christmas party being given by a friend in Athens. I have an animalistic distrust of parties and I almost said no before I realized what I was doing.

It is set for next Friday night, the twenty-sixth, the night after Christmas. I said I would pick her up. She said she had some people she would like me to meet. A very small thrill, I assure them. I played Christmas songs on the stereo all day.

December 21

Something very touching happened today. It was warm enough to be outside and I was watching the wind blow shadows on the lake when Willie, who was throwing rocks near me, suddenly stiffened and took off running. Running up the hill was Carleen. They met and were all over one another, kissing. I felt so happy and sad at the same time. I could not at all tell just what I felt. I felt something was not right in me, that Willie should be doing this when I could not see.

But though I somehow felt it was wrong, I was cheered that after I am gone, there will be someone he will associate with this place, my home. They went off together for about two hours and when he returned, he only smiled, embarrassed. I patted him on the back and asked him if he would like to find a cedar in the woods for a Christmas tree.

We walked west, a direction I rarely walk, crossing the road and the barbed-wire fence of Hiram King and then wandering in a swaying line through the woods. We came to a clearing, and along a fence row, we found about a dozen cedars, and we chopped one off, a small one with my ax. Willie dragged it back through the woods to my house.

I still have some of the decorations Sara made. I found them in a box in the attic, bundled neatly. There was the square one with baubles and the choir scene and the manger scene. We drove to a store and bought lights and a star.

Then we decorated the tree. I asked Willie if they always decorated a tree at his house.

"Sure," he said, looking like I was accusing him of something. "Why?"

"Just asking," I said.

December 22

A cold rain awoke me early this morning. Willie was still asleep. I made strong black coffee and a piece of toast with butter and put on the stereo, softly, Brahms's *Ein Deutches Requiem.*

The yard changes when it rains. The trees, most of the hardwoods, have lost their leaves, and the clouds settled low turning everything the color of ash. I took out my binoculars, the ones I had in Europe during the war. They still work well. I watched the surface of the lake for the beavers, but it was only a pebbled gray as the rain fell. No cranes, either, or other birds. No bird calls. Just a wind like a soft exhalation and the rattle of rain in the brown pile of leaves. And the music.

I always think of Brahms and rain together. Why is that? Is there something about Vienna that is wet and slippery, something beyond Freud?

When I was in my sixties, my right leg used to ache when the rain came in the winter. But I seem to have passed all that. I feel no different in the rain, not even very melancholy, a loss I greatly regret.

Willie awoke about 10:30, but by that time, I had read an article, catalogued fifteen books, and decided what I could buy for his first Christmas with me.

December 23

Willie and I talked about Jesus today. He started things off.

> WILLIE: Jesus was born in a hay barn?
> ANDREW: Maybe it was to show humility.
> WILLIE: Humil . . .
> ANDREW: So he'd be like the plain folks, not putting on fancy airs.
> WILLIE: How could he decide where he would be born?
> ANDREW: Well, he and God are the same person, and God decided ahead of time what would happen.
> WILLIE: That's crazy.
> ANDREW: Why would you say that?
> WILLIE: I can't explain it.
> ANDREW: Neither can I.
> WILLIE: Church is like that.

I mulled later what a strange conversation this was for a few days before Christmas. I drove Willie to Atlanta this afternoon and we bought Christmas presents. I gave him fifty dollars and told him to buy what gifts he wanted for people. When we met two hours later at the mall we visited, he had only one small package and looked pale and drawn.

December 24

I got an intense religious feeling today, almost an epiphany, or something. I have never been religious. Merely another nodding Presbyterian. But this was different, closer. I was watching Willie shoot his BB gun. It was overcast but not too cool.

I was watching the way he held his hands on the gun. His

191

fingers are so thin, almost fragile, but full of grace. And then I could see his hands full of blood and nailed to something hard at the wrists, convulsive, reflexive. And I could not keep myself from seeing it, though I shook my head several times.

When the vision went away, I felt my head full of light, and a buzzing, but melodious feeling kept humming in my head. It was a warm feeling, like being in love. Slowly, it faded. I was breathing hard. Then I felt my arm move and I looked down and Willie was shaking me hard.

"You looked real goofy," he kept saying with some urgency.

"I'm all right," I said, dazed. For the rest of today, I have felt that perhaps God was in me for that moment. Maybe that is what death will be like.

I have not written about Africa lately, but he has grown up sleek and strong, and he hung around me today as if he knew something was after me.

It was almost like something I had felt before, like the warmth of Sara's touch in the darkness.

December 25

I gave Willie: pants, shirts, socks, underwear, shoes, a turquoise ring, two models, computer football game, other stuff.

Willie gave me: a tie tack and a copy of *Fighting Indians of the Old West* by Dee Brown. In the front of the book, he wrote this: "You will like this Doc. From Willie."

Later, Bill McAdam dropped by and was baffled by Willie, though he admitted he knew the real story and that I had lied to him this summer. He didn't seem to care. Bill brought me a fifth of bourbon, a gift from himself and his father. I had Bill's gift ready, the first-edition copy of *The Sea around Us* I had kept all these years. He was very grateful. Later, between singing Christmas songs with Willie and drinking some, I called my sister and told her I would be up for the wedding on the thirtieth as planned, but that I was bringing somebody with me. When I told Willie, he was very excited and a little scared.

I tried to get the feeling I had yesterday, but no luck. Still, the best Christmas in years. Very happy.

December 26

I took a long walk today to ruddy up my face for my tryst with Hannah tonight. I asked Willie to come with me, but he said no, he wanted to walk back up to his old house by himself. I told him what I'd heard, that everything had been sold, and that they were planning to tear down the house because the county inspector condemned it. He nodded glumly.

I did not feel completely well. I feel like something is hidden just below the ribs on my right side, hidden down inside me, waiting, with eyes, to be found. But I did not feel too badly so I tried to walk several miles.

There is a joy in feeling your muscles fill up, of taking long strides in breath-feather weather. To my surprise, I saw a fox dashing across a trail near me, a thin, angular fellow with a bushy tail. The fox was peach colored, smooth and silky, and nimble as a bug.

When I got back to the house, I was terribly tired and feared I would be too worn out to see Hannah. But after a nap, I showered and felt much better, and then I sat down here and wrote in my journal. Ah, such dedication.

December 27

I bought the tickets for the flight today, calling the airport. Willie was full of questions about flying, mainly crashes.

"I seen that one on TV where the little plane flew into the big one and killed all them people," he said.

"That was pretty bad."

"Think we'll get killed?"

"Don't be ridiculous. It's safer to fly than to drive."

"But you can't have no fender bender in a jet plane."

He had me there. But I calmed him and told him about where we would be flying, to Boston, then on a connector to Hyannis. He seemed like a soldier facing a tough situation, resigned to his fate, but almost a little excited.

Hannah was . . . She treated me like an old man.

December 28

Virlyn called today and we had a long talk. Then Louis called and said he was going into the hospital, that they think he might have something in the small intestine. Sounded ominous.

Then Hannah called. Her voice was slightly frayed, like yarn scraping something. She said she was sorry that we didn't have a better time.

"It's okay," I said. "You probably don't go out with fossils all that often."

"But you're not a fossil," she cried. Then she said a lot of embarrassing things, either myopic or dishonest, probably the former, because in her I find no malice.

I couldn't help thinking of Callie and her straight answers and the nights we spent in Wyoming. I mollified Hannah as I could and told her I would see her soon. Then I dialed Callie's number and when her maid picked up the phone with her formal, round tones, I quietly laid the receiver in the cradle.

I cannot decide whether I prefer charitable lies or the awful truth, the darkness.

December 29

We spent much of the day packing, and I felt excited and happy to be seeing my sister again. It has been five years. That was at Sara's funeral I saw her last.

Actually, I have never liked flying that much. The first time was in 1928 in a biplane in Kansas. I'll not forget that soon, and I felt like my breath would not come back and I kept laughing the whole time and I couldn't stop. The man took me up to about 1,500 feet and then nosedived and pulled out about 300 feet off the ground.

I fainted. When I came around, we were rising slightly over a fence row, and I felt joyous to be alive and when we finally set down, I was exhilarated. But after a while, I began to shake a little, thinking about it, then I got to shivering all over, and then I got sick.

The pilot, who flew in an aerial circus, just laughed like a mule when I threw up. I didn't think that was fair. Always, after that, I thought of coming down so fast your teeth hurt and then there was this funny feeling behind your eyes and then you passed out cold.

Willie has been quiet all day. He sits and stares out the window sometimes. Hums sometimes. I wonder if he is doing what I did the next time after I flew with the aerial circus: making peace with his tormentors and love to his indiscretions.

December 30

We are high over the East Coast. Below us, Chesapeake Bay snakes and elbows up the coast, grand and beautiful. I like their oysters.

Willie has a silly grin on his face, and he wouldn't sit on the window, so I did. I've had three of those little bottles of whiskey. We could go down now and I wouldn't mind too much. But I'm proud of the boy. Here's what happened earlier.

"We're off the ground, Doc."

"That's what you do in an airplane."

"How high do we go?"

"How high do you think?"

"A hundred miles."

Maybe we are now, I don't know. I am one sorry son of a bitch to be in this condition, but I love drinking on airplanes second only to writing on airplanes. Actually, I've finished some of my best monographs on airplanes. Look at that stewardess. She leans over and I nudge Willie and point at her ass. He starts grinning all over, his whole face is grinning and I know everything is all right.

Ah, the father and son. How touching! I wish we could fly a hundred miles up in the sky. I wish we could pull an Icarus into the sun.

We'll be on the Cape by midafternoon, and the wedding isn't until eight tonight. (Weird time for a wedding.) Willie keeps leaning over and trying to read this. I quit.

January 1

Bitterly cold, snow blowing in the air, the feeling of damp salt on your skin. I am sitting at the kitchen table of my sister's house. Everyone else is still in bed. It's only 6:30.

The wedding was fine, and we stayed up until 1 A.M. partying and drinking champagne. My nephew Paul got horribly drunk and started saying bawdy things about Claire. She was mildly amused at first, but then turned crimson. Paul hinted she had never had an orgasm, and I don't blame her for being furious. After all, they're in their forties.

But I awoke early with sleet rapping on my window upstairs. Willie was asleep beside me, but did not stir when I got up. Now, the sleet has changed to snow, small, spitting flakes.

The reception of Willie has been curious. At first, most everybody treated it like a miracle, but later I felt (and I fear Willie did) that he was just an ignorant interloper who could observe but not share.

Maybe I'm just being overly sensitive.

I walked out to the barn and got some wood and started a nice fire. Today is New Year's Day and the football games will be on television and I'm sure my sister will need some help around the house.

I was unsure, at one time, if I would make it to this year. But though I rate my chances of being around for another New Year slim (maybe 15 percent) I'll try to make it.

But I'll die before I take chemotherapy. I saw what it did to somebody I loved and she died anyway.

But those are lachrymal words. I'll not be a merchant of that today, not this whitening morning. The fire is crackling now and I can hear people starting to move upstairs. I enjoy their company, but there is a mortal blessing in solitude.

Bless this wedding. We will fly back tomorrow.

Later. We now have four inches of snow on the ground and it is coming down harder. This much snow is unusual for the Cape. My feet are thawing out. I took Willie out. They have, in the barn, three real Flexible Flyer sleds. The hill behind the house that slopes off to the woods is covered by neighborhood kids. I put Willie on the slope, lying on the sled and kicked him off down the long hill.

He screamed with delight. When he came dragging back up the hill, he was turned all into a smile, it seemed.

"Doc, this is right wonderful."

I kicked him downhill again. He's still out there, even though it is getting dark. Most everybody has eaten and drunk too much today, but I have been rather Spartan.

Is this the beginning of some new resolution?

January 2

The snow clouds evaporate below us and suddenly we are over the mountains of Pennsylvania. Willie is sitting on the window. This is an Eastern flight and the windows aren't as clean as the Delta we had coming up.

Willie is not scared anymore. He looks different. Not just the new clothes I bought him or his hair. He looks almost like a dreamy young romantic, believing anything is possible, hoping that the terrible will thrill him in some dark way.

I know. When I was a young man, I read *The Sorrows of Young Werther* and plotted suicide for a long time. Not seriously, but as an exercise in humility and sacrifice.

Should I consider suicide again, now that I am out of romances and fevers in the blood? What way would I choose. Back then, nearly sixty years ago, I had it all worked out. I would slit my wrists. That would be neat and when I cut the veins and arteries, I would lean forward on my desk with my cheek on a copy of something like *Werther*, and with my last statement and the quill with which it was written close by. It would be a masterpiece of false diffidence.

If I were to do it now, if things got so bad, I would probably use a gun. I like the idea of exploding out of the world. But I would probably be the same coward at that time. No, I will curl in my bed and know, at the end, that I would never get out of it again, and that I would lie there until I awoke into another spring.

January 3

Home. Willie took off for a visit with Carleen and said he would be gone all night. I scolded him as best I could, but it did no good, and I found myself asking something that made me blush down to my toes.

"Have you got any protection?" I blurted.

"I ain't scared of nothing," he answered quizzically. I tried to think of some proper euphemism. No luck.

"I mean rubbers," I said. "Have you got any rubbers?"

He laughed a little in a kind of choke and coughed a little.

"She makes me take it out," he muttered.

By this time, I could not even look at him any more. I patted him on the shoulder and walked away in a sweat. Why is it so hard to admit our natural urges? We hide them, disguise them, and then we try to forgive ourselves for them, when all along it's what we think about the most.

That kind of morality is the penance we pay for having made sacraments of our personal mysteries.

January 4

I took Willie to church today at the Calvary Baptist Church. He didn't want to go. I made him.

Everyone was nice, and I was astounded when the preacher spoke on the Prodigal Son. All through the service, I watched Willie out of the corner of my eye. He was breathing too hard. And he kept looking around him as if he expected everyone to regard him as unfit to be there.

But later, he began to calm down, and by the time the final hymn came, he was singing along with me in a kind of flat, off-key baritone. After we got home, he was quiet for a long time while I cooked roast beef for him.

January 5

Willie started to school today.

I feel poorly. Hurting.

January 6

This pain in my side.

January 12

I am in Athens General Hospital, have been for four days now. Willie came home last Tuesday afternoon and found me on the floor, unconscious. Even now, I shake when I try to sit up too long.

Willie brought me my journal. The nurse won't let me write much longer. All they say is they're doing tests. No visitors yet. Don't know who sent all the flowers.

January 13

Feeling much better today. Willie was taken by Callie and kept at her house. I feel a little angry about that. Dr. Rowley came in this morning and sat on the edge of the bed with a chart in his hand and said I had a case of pneumonia along with the cancer. He seemed surprised that it hadn't spread any farther than it had. He treated me for it earlier.

They're pumping me full of stuff. Had me out walking up and down the hall. Getting my strength back.

Visitors tomorrow.

January 14

Callie came over with Willie. My breathing is stronger and I am eating like a horse. Dr. Rowley is amazed my cancer hasn't proved him a seer.

Callie very shyly asked me how I felt, and I said good. She looked very pretty and I wished I could take back every bad thing I ever thought about her. Her eyes were soft, as if photographed through gauze.

"And when are you coming home?" she asked.

"When the doctor releases me."

"Willie's being good."

"Thank heavens for small favors."

"He misses you."

"I miss him."

"I miss you."

I reached out my hand to her and she sat on the edge of the bed. I was worried about my breath and my hair was not clean. But I pulled her to me and kissed her anyway, and she was trembling a little.

Willie came in after Callie went out, bundled in a coat I had not seen. He said Callie bought it for him.

"Boy, you hit the jackpot, huh," I needled him.

"I'm going to ask her for a Corvette next," he grinned.

"You been good?"

"If I get any better, I ain't gonna be able to stand myself."

"That's funny."

"You feeling okay, Doc?"

"Don't call me Doc."

"Okay. You feeling okay?"

"Better," I nodded hopefully. He pressed my hand and turned to leave.

Over his shoulder, he said, "Doc, you know it ain't long till spring." I started to say something to him, but then he was gone. Then I took a nap and they walked me down the hall and I came back and wrote this.

January 15

Why do I always try to order things, to categorize? Do I believe that history is so ordered because I have lived through all those ages in my studies and teaching? History is disordered, does not repeat itself. Human failures repeat themselves, failures and joys.

And so I repeat myself always, the feeling I get when I look out this hospital window over the rooftops, how I felt watching Sara sink into herself under the luxuriance of flowers each day, how I saw my mother quietly smile into her passing, also.

I thought I was dying when I fell down last week. But it was cold and it hurt and I was sick, and I have always believed death to be warm, maternal, and like being swallowed by warm earth.

And so I repeat the silly surmise that somehow my passing will shake some foundation. That the roots will tremble under the trees. But no. The earth only shook once when a man died, and since then, most people have forgotten why.

I am tired, happy.

January 16

Hannah came by today. She had a little blue handkerchief, all knotted up, like the heroine of an old romance. It seemed more like a prop than anything useful. She laughed too hard at everything I said. I wished I could have locked the door and slid her under the covers with me.

I guess I'm getting a little callous now that I'm feeling better.

I had a surprise visit from Professor Thomas Andrews. He taught me history when I was in school. He must be over ninety now, but he still goes to his office every day and works on papers.

"You look awful," he said in a raspy voice, but he was smiling.

"You look like death warmed over, too," I said maliciously, and he laughed out loud.

"Death's given up on me," he shrugged. "I can't say I'm worth all that much."

"I can't say I'm worth all that much, either. I feel pretty good."

"What you got? I got diabetes, high blood pressure, and glaucoma. And, oh, yeah, I got . . ." he searched for the answer. "Oh, yeah, I got hemmorhoids, got them things."

"I got high blood pressure, cancer, and pneumonia."

"Holy Jesus, I know death won't take us," he said. We chatted amiably for a few minutes and then, abruptly, he stood straight up and bowed like a Viennese tailor and turned on his heels and was gone.

January 17

I thought I could go home today, but no, they said not yet, maybe tomorrow. They keep coming and going, shuttling around me, sticking me with syringes and then plucking them out like a filling-station attendant yawningly removing the gas nozzle from a car. I don't mean anything to them. That's how they manage to go home at night.

I admire Callie tremendously for helping out with Willie. She brought him over again this afternoon late, just after he got out of school. I asked him what he learned today, but he said nothing.

"Nothing? Then why did you go to school?" I asked.

"I got to," he grinned.

"You better get it in gear, because when I get home, I'm going to quiz you on your lessons."

"She don't do that," he said, gesturing at Callie.

"She *doesn't* do that. Who's teaching you grammar?"

"An old lady."

"Grammar's the same as it was when she was your age."

"When she was my age there was dinosaurs in the pasture."

I couldn't help it. He made me laugh. While he roamed outside waiting, Callie sat with me for a while, and I could tell from her eyes that she cares for me. There is no vanity in this assertion.

January 18

I measure things in shades. There is no drama in my life, other than this silly miracle play of my mortal misfortune.

There is nothing like the Cooper's hawk with its broad wings drooping under a dying summer sun to pick a mouse from a trough in the broomsedge. Nothing like that.

There is nothing like the great movements of battle or the throbbing moments of first love in a terrified seclusion. I cannot pretend the grandeur of slapping a sorrel mare over the Great Plains, a travois trailing behind, and in the distance, the smoky smudge of campfires against the broad-backed sky.

There are lives that make background music, like the humming of cellos against the violin's solo. These are the minor figures whose power never exceeds their desire, who give little and live happily. Shall we place on them the mantle of ignorance because they have lived too little or none too well?

If so, place that mantle around my old shoulders now. I have found nothing of note under a microscope, nor have I seen any truths that were not seen under the timeless blue sky of Greece. But I have felt sometimes in the darkness the breath of passion that pushes me dazed through a world of splendor and terror and poverty and riches. I have never understood it all, but I have gloried in its riches and trembled in its light.

January 19

I will go home tomorrow. The real problem, they tell me, is my susceptibility to disease. My cancer seems to be in remission, though they claim this is unusual without any therapy at all. I got in a good shot at Dr. Rowley.

"You think the only way a man can be cured is through

your medicine and without it, he will surely die. You sound like a shaman rattling bones and stones around a campfire.''

''Science, Dr. Lachlan, not superstition,'' he said, seeming quite amused.

''If I need your science, then why am I still alive?''

''I can't answer that. Maybe God can.''

''And you talk about science?'' He shrugged and I laughed out loud.

''Hell, you'll probably outlive me,'' he said. That was a bad lie, but it made him feel better and I did not really care. I feel wonderful, though in a little pain. But my head is clear, and he said my lungs appear to be holding up.

I'm ready to begin my survey of the pond all over again. I need to find my own geography. It will help me learn. That's what I'm trying to do.

January 20

Willie and I talked about war today when we got home. He is worried about having to go to war one day. He has been studying war at school. He asked me about how it was to be in the war.

''It was bad,'' I said simply.

''*Real* bad?''

''I had a friend named Tyler,'' I continued. ''We were in Sicily. That's an island south of Italy. Anyway, we were huddled up against this building and snipers were letting us have it. I had a squad. Tyler wasn't too far from me. I was watching the snipers chip corners off the concrete when all of a sudden Tyler just kind of slumped over where he was like he was taking a nap. I scrambled over to him. He'd been hit in the side of the head. Killed instantly. Nothing in my life, well almost nothing, ever hurt more than that. You wanted to do something, but there was nothing, nothing."

"I'm sorry, Doc," he said sadly. "He was your friend?"

"Oh, yeah. War doesn't have any glamor but to old men, Willie. By then, most of them have forgotten."

"You think we'll have a war soon?"

"When it's time for a war, it just happens. It takes a lifetime of stupidity and sloth and greed to get a good one going. We may be heading there, but we're not there yet."

I wish I could describe how Willie's eyes looked when we were talking about this. I felt sad for him, a little hurt and I also felt an abiding love.

January 21

No more temporal things. I am going to learn about the world around me. But I don't want to conk out before spring, so I won't go outside today, since it is raining and sleeting and bitterly cold.

When Willie went to school this morning, I made sure he had money for his lunch. I gave him five dollars for a fifty-cent lunch. That's ridiculous. I'm going to ruin his sense of money, of which he has little anyway.

I played with his race-car set a little this morning. Had a dandy time. Then I read from the *Federalist Papers,* then some Wordsworth, and finally from a book about the American Plains.

By the time Willie came home, I was starting supper, the fire was hot and the rain had turned into snow.

January 22

School was canceled today because of the snow. It is wet, about six inches deep, and the world outside my house is deep and silent, as if a cave had edged over the forest and Shadow Pond as we slept.

I bundled up as best I could and walked down to the pond with Willie. The snow had stopped, but a bitterly cold wind was sweeping in from the northwest and the edges of the pond had frozen. The surface of the water was like a mirror, and even the wind that rippled it could not dispel that tired comparison for me.

There is a soft benevolence in southern snow. But I could not share it. Willie hit me in the back of the head with a huge, dripping ball of sleet and snow. When I turned to roar at him, he had turned tail and ducked behind a tree, laughing in bursts like machine-gun fire.

I grabbed a ball of slush and put it behind my back.

"How can you do that to a sick old man?" I asked sadly.

When he came out sheepishly from behind the tree, I waited until he was close enough and smacked him right in the face. He shook all over and started to get mad, and then he started laughing again and picked up another handful of snow.

I ran to him before he could throw it and pinned his shoulders to his side and fell with him into the snow.

Now, evening has come early, and Willie is keeping a good fire going. I have soup on the stove and it smells wonderful.

Maybe we did share some of that benevolence.

January 23

I am a fool, helpless.

When I awoke in the middle of the night last night, I walked into the kitchen to get some milk and I heard voices. I followed them and found they were coming from Willie's room.

I listened, putting my ear to the floor. He had closed the trap door leading to his room, though there was no longer any need for it. It was Carleen. They were talking quietly, and I could only sometimes hear the words.

If I were doing what I should, I would rip the door from its hinges and hurl the most morally outraged invective possible down upon them like God from Mount Sinai. But I only felt something different, something that was confusing and painful.

I crept back to my bed and felt sorry for myself. There was nothing in me to chastise Willie, no guilt or rage or moral suasion. I had said nothing before. But here in my house? Is that how I want him to behave? Would they take him away from me if they knew?

I do not know how to tell him his love is mistaken, that what he is doing is reserved for those who are married or that he does not understand the nature of love at all.

I wish one thing: that it didn't hurt me. I wish I could challenge what I feel. I wish I could bless them in my home.

Later. When I awoke, I remembered how I had felt during the night, but she had gone and I did not betray my feelings to Willie. He went outside and chopped wood and in an hour, he had stripped to his T-shirt and worked up a sweat. Most of the snow is gone.

Nothing lasts long in this season.

January 24

I miss teaching Willie. Maybe I just miss teaching. I looked back over my copy of the book I wrote on Carrington. I remember teaching a course on the West for the first time and getting intrigued with the movements of troops and with Red Cloud's War.

Then Dee Brown came out with *Fort Phil Kearny* and I made it required reading. From that, I got interested in Carrington. The copy of my book on Carrington is now falling loose at the signatures. And I marked it all up, both with corrections and extra thoughts.

I could have done it better. I could, if they'd go another printing. Not much hope for that. It is terrifying at first to see all your stupidities permanently in print.

But then you don't worry about it so much. At least I did something. At least I looked at one man's life and got close enough to hear his words.

I feel like writing a lot today. Why is that? Maybe it's the birds that are crying and singing outside. The weather is warmer.

I have been reflective since I was sick. I need to push again, into something besides this prattle. I know something is there. I have to achieve something.

I must prove there is some order.

January 25

Met Callie at church in town. When I took her home, we sat on her couch and began kissing. It lasted for some time.

Then we sat apart and it seemed like we were brooding over something. We were silent.

It happened quickly.

"Let's get married," she said. My mouth fell open.

"Are you serious?"

"Sure."

"But you never even said you love me," I said. I wanted to say yes then, but I stopped myself.

"Do you love me?"

"I'm not sure," I said tentatively.

"Oh, great," she said. "I propose and you don't know if you love me. Great." She seemed twenty years younger. Maybe a little like Hannah. I wanted to smile but I wouldn't let myself.

"Do you love me?" I asked.

"Yes. Yes." She nodded gently.

"You sure you don't just want me for my retirement?"

"I've got more money than *you'll* ever see," she harrumphed.

We talked on for about an hour, but I couldn't say yes and I couldn't say I love her. Maybe I don't love her. Maybe I need to spend out my days alone with Willie. What would he do with another senior citizen around the house?

But maybe I should accept Callie. She would warm my bed and talk with me in front of the fire at night and we could tour the world on her money. Tour the world!

Why do things like this happen to me? Why? Jesus Christ!

January 26

I lay awake half the night thinking about it all. There is one ghost I cannot thrust away. Like a maudlin old maid I keep wanting Sara's advice on all this. I respected her opinion. Not mine all that much in matters of love. I could never find how love had given anything of value in history. Sara would snort angrily when I said that. She was a romantic.

But I suppose I am, too, and now that I am pressed against some old feelings made new, I know again how I fear what I cannot control.

There is something that bothers me terribly about Callie having proposed. At my age, I should have escaped such formalities years ago. But there is some sanity in structure, as I have always believed, and this method disturbs.

It is the dark season of the year now. Outside, heavy clouds settle down over the house. The smoke from the fire lingers down over the windows. The draft is not good.

It is Monday. Willie has gone to school. In history, he is studying the Age of Reason. But when he gets older he will find there was no such thing. Ages are guided by the heart and the genitals.

I don't know what to do.

January 27

I discussed the matter with Willie last night. He was full of pep. I kept trying to remember how he looked last May. He doesn't look like that anymore. He thinks I should marry Callie, even though he doesn't really know her.

"But I won't have as much time for you," I said. He laughed.

"So what?"

"Don't you care?"

"No." He thought about it. "I mean I care and all, but you got a life, too. I ain't trying to wrap you up or nothing."

217

I do got a life, too. Maybe we could travel. Maybe we could make a better home for Willie. Maybe I could find all sorts of excuses not to admit I am lonely and old.

January 28

We met at the Country Pine. The place looked deserted, almost as if Callie had arranged for no one else to be there. We ate a large lunch.

"I accept your offer," I said, lighting a cigar.

"Phew, don't smoke those things," she said.

"Ah, Xantippe, becoming a shrew already?"

"I'm sorry, Andrew," she said. She put her head in her hands and leaned on the table.

"Well? I said I accept."

"Aren't you going to propose properly?"

"You already did that."

"Oh, come on." She was grinning and I did not feel badly, sort of amused but a little embarrassed.

"Okay, Callie, will you marry me?"

"No," she said. I did not flinch.

"Why not? Is it the cigar?"

"You haven't said you love me."

That caught me unprepared. I looked at her and tried to keep smiling, but first my mouth then my eyes turned down. This was a serious question, much more serious than getting married. But I had to be honest. The problem was that I didn't entirely know what I felt.

"I need you," I said tentatively, looking around to see if anyone were listening. No one else was in the restaurant but the waitress and the cashier. "And I miss you when we're not together. And I think you are the kindest, most caring person I know.''

''I love you, too,'' she said. It all seemed kind of silly, but it didn't feel that way. I felt deeply touched.

We set the date for Sunday, March 1, in her church in town.

When I told Willie, he congratulated me. Only then did I realize that we have not discussed where we will live, or what we shall do, or the relationship I have with Willie.

January 29

Yahoo! I feel drunk with happiness! I feel like writing exclamation points after everything I write! If I wrote ''It was the best of times, it was the worst of times!'' I would end that with an exclamation mark!

Willie and I went fishing today! We caught several bream! I cleaned them and cooked them for us and showed Willie how to make hushpuppies!

I talked with Callie on the phone this morning! I told her that we could talk about where we would live after the wedding! She said she always wanted to live out here with me! I told her that was the best news I'd had! She said we would rent out her big house for a fabulous amount!

I asked her frankly about her income! She gets a pension, but it isn't needed! From her father's stocks, she gets an income of $7,000 a month! But we could double that if we needed to!

She said for a honeymoon, she'd like to cruise around the world! Can we afford that?! Of course we can, she said!

I love you, I said! I wondered if that admission was moti-

vated by all this financial good news! That's a terrible
thought! But nothing is terrible now!

Yahoo!

January 30

I just re-read what I wrote yesterday. I feel a bit more mellow now, but no less happy. Today is my birthday.

I took a long walk deep into the woods today, far away
from the trails. The day was cold, but there was no wind and
I wrapped up tightly. I came out of the woods at one point
onto a rolling pasture, cropped close from a herd of Holsteins. There were rocks and pebbles littered in places,
washed up from hoofing and rains.

Suddenly I felt something strange, not a physical sensa-
tion, but a rush of intuitive knowledge. I felt as if something
in nature had accepted me and was sharing its wordless wisdom. I looked around me, certain I was being watched, but
there were only the stands of pine and the low brambles,
unmoving in the weak light.

There was a sense of ease and grace along the hills and
through the forest. There was no anger or fear in anything.
And then I realized that I, also, felt no anger or fear, not of
life or death or from the sky or the sea or the earth. I could
almost feel my arms turning into branches and my feet into
chunks of cracked chert and quartz.

I took a long time walking home, dazed by my fortune,
thanking God that I had lived long enough for this hour.

January 31

Willie and I drove to Atlanta today to hear a concert by a string quartet. He was very apprehensive, and instead of asking him, I tried to consider why.

But Willie relaxed when we entered the concert hall, and he sat politely and tried to read the program, his finger bumping unevenly along under the words.

They played quartets by Haydn and Beethoven. I immensely enjoyed them, and Willie seemed alternately absorbed and embarrassed for some reason.

Afterward, I took him to a steak house and he ate with much gusto and talked about baseball without stopping. I asked him what he thought of the concert and he said it was good. That was all.

My health on the last day of January is remarkably good. The pain in my side has gone. My breathing is good. I feel strong. Maybe I can last even for some years.

In this good mood, I stopped at a large department store in a mall on the way home and bought Willie one hundred dollars' worth of assorted happiness.

February 1

I am determined to refine my desires. What is it that determines which foods a person enjoys? Conditioning? Or is it
some hereditary chemistry in the tongue?

I will write down here my favorite foods. Maybe I can understand something about myself then, something more. In
no special order: peanut butter, pork and beans, steak, dark
bread, bran flakes, ice cream with Hershey's syrup, potato
chips, chicken gumbo soup, apples, broccoli, fried potatoes, cheese (mild cheddar is best), milk, lettuce, colored
butter beans, Stroganoff, hamburgers, hot dogs, spaghetti,
toast with real butter, pickles, eggs, bacon, sausage, field
peas, apple butter, ham, hash browns, grits, coffee, fish.

The most inedible things currently considered food in-
clude: asparagus (the worst, ghastly), green onion potato
chips, mayo, olives, and chicken livers.

I can make nothing whatever of the preceding.

February 2

Willie and Africa have become great pals. I watched out the
window this morning when Willie left to walk to the bus
stop. There was a slight wind waving Willie's dark hair and
ruffling Africa's coat. Willie kept turning around and
gesturing for Africa to stay put, but he kept creeping after
Willie. I watched Willie's frustration grow. Usually, Africa

stays on the porch. Why does he want to leave today? I went on to the porch and called Africa.

He came bounding back to me, his entire back wagging. But as he wagged, he kept glancing over his back at Willie, watching him recede down the dirt road.

"You respect me, but you love him," I said to Africa.

Africa looked at me admiringly, respectfully. I have never been able to understand the canine prerogative. Later, I happened to pass the window and I saw Africa rolling happily in a pile of leaves, kicking them up into the cold air.

February 3

I am aghast at all the details that need to be worked out for the wedding. I do not remember all that with Sara. But then it's never the way you remember it. Callie came out today and we talked about it all rather clinically.

"I don't want to send out invitations and have people there."

"We've got to, you jerk," she said. "My family still lives hereabouts."

That's something else I don't know much about. How will her family take this? Will they consider me just a silver-haired gold digger?

"Probably," she said cheerfully.

I told her maybe we should just consider getting married by the justice of the peace. Maybe no formal ceremony.

"What are you afraid of?" she asked. Nothing, I assured her. Who is going to be my best man? Charles. I'll ask him.

Who is going to give her away? Her brother Howard who lives in Archer.

What if somebody in the congregation objects and won't forever hold his peace?

"Will you please stop being an old maid," she said, exasperated.

I tried sulking, but that didn't work. I'm just stink happy about it all. I don't care what she plans. Just point me in the right direction.

February 4

A gray day, a day for sadness. Bill McAdam's father, Tom, was working late in his store last night on inventory, he and a clerk. Suddenly Tom just plopped down on the floor, dead.

Heart attack. He was only fifty-five.

I went over to the house this morning and Bill was sitting in the front parlor, neat in a dark suit, his hair parted cleanly. He was holding a Kleenex that was stiff as parchment and his eyes were ringed and red.

I hugged him and he started crying again. His mother couldn't come out. She was under a doctor's care. There were people all over the place. Bill and I went on the back porch to get some air. He felt better then.

We talked about fishing and how his father had taken him to the coast and how they went deer hunting this year and that his dad had promised to take him elk hunting in Wyoming this fall. I can't remember our conversation. I was too upset to record it like I usually do.

But I told him how sorry I am and that I would do any-

thing for him I could. Then he asked me if I would be a pallbearer and I said I would be honored.

I have never done that before, am scared to do it.

February 5

Callie's been giving me hell about being a pallbearer if I
didn't want to be one.

"I do, I just feel funny about it," I said. "I don't like
being that close to a dead person."

"That's positively medieval," she snorted.

"Actually, it's natural to be uneasy around dead folks," I
said.

"Don't give me that scholarly *noblesse oblige,*" she said
sternly.

She was right. I didn't have any business complaining.

I am a stranger around it. I always avoided it. But I remember the war too well. I was beginning to lose the feelings of respect and awe I had for the dead. I was getting too
comfortable with it. That's what frightened me.

I am not cut out to dwell on the mysteries of the other
side.

February 6

It's all over. It was an easy job, with six other men I did not
know. We only carried it a few feet. Everyone took it badly.

When I got home, I had a stiff drink and sat before a fire, waiting for Willie to come home.

By all accounts, he was a good man, a reasonable parent, and a strong husband. There must be some order to his early death, some reason that he is now under the wind-swept redness of the Branton City Cemetery.

I have borne to rest a man I never knew. Perhaps it is better that way. At least I never knew him truly. Yet I have shared in the grief of his passing, not as a friend or lover, but as another man who has tried to love the seasons well, to drink a glass to the health of a child, and to sing as long as God allowed.

There is no injustice in being mourned by those you loved, and those you hoped loved you. Somewhere, I am convinced his shade has seen us all come into his absence with love. Somewhere, I am convinced, he has been comforted, as have we all.

February 7

The woods are changed today. A cushion of sleet has rattled down in the night, and there is about four inches of it this morning. There is no wind, as if the land were holding its breath, waiting for what comes next.

Sleet makes the land harsher than snow, but it also makes the change less ephemeral. A crunch, not a mush. I watched through the kitchen window for a long while, and presently a blue jay landed in the ice and began to search for food. I called to Willie, who took a few bread heels outside and crumbled them where the blue jay had landed.

We made some coffee and watched. First, the chickadees came, then the sparrows and the cardinals, and then the blue jays. The blue jays blustered around and tried to intimidate the others. Finally, a large pileated woodpecker dropped among them, and even the blue jays scattered to nearby branches to wait.

Willie was much taken by the spectacle and I told him about the natural pecking order, about dominance and survival and territoriality. Probably I got some of it wrong, but mostly I got it right.

We decided, late in the morning, to take a walk in the woods. The edge of Shadow Pond was frozen over with sleet, and occasionally, a flapping duck would explode from the water into lowstrung clouds. Africa bounded along happily with us.

Perhaps sleet is better than snow, at least in the country. There are no grotesque snowmen staring back with coal eyes or sooty piles in huge chunks along the road. It is cold, clear, and you feel it under foot. It has substance.

While we were walking, a wind rose from the east, and huge snowflakes, the size of plums began to tumble on us. Willie tried to catch one in his mouth and so did I. I could have sworn they tasted sweet, as if they had been soaking in sugared milk. I asked Willie, but he shrugged.

Now, it is the afternoon and the snow has stopped and it is very still once more. I think about Napoleon's retreat from Moscow, perhaps Valley Forge or the Cheyennes camped on the Washita as Custer and his troops moved in to murder them.

All kinds of historical allusions. But they pass quietly. Willie is sitting near the fire, curled into an afghan Sara made, trying to read a tattered copy of *Light of the Western Stars* by Zane Grey.

February 8

Willie's room is too cold now, even with the heater. He is sleeping in bed with me, under the luxury of my electric blanket. I feel somewhat self-conscious, but it is nice to feel someone stir at my side during the bitter cold of the nights.

For the first time this season, water froze on the inside of the windows last night. I don't understand the physics of the situation.

Willie and I talked for some time after we went to bed last night. Again, he startled me with his frankness.

"Doc, do women like screwing or do they just go along with it?"

"They like it, maybe not as much as men." That may have been wrong. How the hell do I know?

"But you don't quit when you get to be . . . older?"

"No, not if you're physically able."

"I didn't know that."

"I didn't either when I was a young man."

I steered us away from such talk. I don't even remember seeing my mother's legs. What kind of tutor could I be in love? A poor one. He was quiet for some time.

"Duke's mayonnaise is better than Kraft's," he said suddenly.

"Why'd you say that?" I asked.

"Because it's true," he said.

February 9

Today I . . . Oh hell, I don't want to write today.

February 10

Depressed, evil feeling.

February 11

Begin again, I have got to stop this silly, fearful pity. I am heartily sick of winter and ready for bright sunshine, a slight breeze, and a rod and reel in my hand. We are almost housebound by the sleet, the muck now. The sleet is no longer welcome. It has turned mostly to a thick, gooey mud, and the only whiteness left huddles in the corners, away from the weak-kneed sun.

I talked to Callie on the phone today. She was fussing at me for being diffident, challenging me to quit wasting away and start on a new monograph, even a book. I told her I would like to but my mental energy is low.

"That's a sophist's phrase for laziness," she chided. Okay, I told her, I'll try to do better. Even Willie is worried about me. He brought me home a pint of bourbon. When I started to question him sternly about where he got such a thing, he smiled and wouldn't say anything. So I quit.

Damn the way I feel! Damn it!

February 12

Willie left yesterday just at dark and was gone all night. This morning, I called the school and asked to speak to him and he was there, to my surprise. I was furious.

"Where in the hell were you last night?"

"I was visiting somebody," he said.

"In this weather?" I shouted. I was red.

"It was warm."

"Who were you visiting?"

"None of your business."

"You little jerk, who do you think you are?"

"Don't you know yet?" he asked, hanging up on me. I wanted to drive over to the school and get him, but I said I was through with this sort of thing.

Why is his respect so erratic? Where is he going? Why in the *hell* can't I be more commanding?

I know the answers. He is here for my amusement as I am here for his. We are sharing a playbook, from which each of us reads an idiot's lines. But we are all characters, never remembering who we were last.

Sometimes, our shadows cross and we know that neither has the right to sanctity.

February 13

Willie came home about the middle of the evening last night, and I was shocked at how he looked, dirty, disheveled, with weak, unfocused eyes. He poured a tall glass of milk and made a peanut butter sandwich and sat in the den with his legs across the arms of a wing chair, munching silently.

I asked him was it Callie. He shrugged. It ain't nothing, he said. Why are you treating me like this, then?

"I ain't treating you like nothing," he said.

"Would you like to go live with Virlyn in Covington?" I asked bluntly. I had not prepared the question and it struck me like a mallet on a disc of bronze. I vibrated with the question's resonance.

"He's old and sick," Willie said, his voice softer, more vulnerable than perhaps in recent days.

"And I'm Charles Atlas?" I said. Willie looked puzzled and I knew he didn't know what I was talking about.

"I don't think so," he said. Then he looked down and said okay, which I took to mean he would try to straighten up.

"Okay," I said.

February 14

Despair is somehow mixed up with love. One of its attendants. You expect nothing so fine to last until sunrise. When the moon swells up over your house and she is there beside you, no hate or pain is near. But when the songbirds begin their notes down through the sun-littered woods, it starts again, this brief death of hope, and then despair.

February 15

A shade of spring today? Callie and I met at her house this morning to discuss details. She had the curtains pulled back and the sun, stronger, poured in across the fine rugs and into our laps as we sat near an empty fireplace.

Her brother Howard will give her away, she said. Howard dropped by while we were talking and though I knew he was younger than she, I wasn't prepared for the fact that he is only fifty-four and looks no older than forty.

I told Callie how I feel about Willie, about how I had sat for hours the other day, staring at the marshy edge of the pond, trying to understand how ill prepared I am to be a father.

She sat close to me on the couch and put her head on my shoulder and I felt happy and she said that she would help me work things out. This match is already helping my disposition.

We spent several hours talking about a wedding trip. She wants to take a cruise around the world, but I have rather resisted spending that much money, as I don't want her friends to see me as a white-haired gigolo.

Lately, I have been thinking about something more modest, such as a trip to the Florida Keys. I've always wanted to go there, and when I mentioned it to Callie, she was intrigued.

February 16

So warm that this afternoon when Willie came home from school, we walked down to the edge of Shadow Pond and went fishing. We made small talk for a little while. I watched his grace in fascination as he cast out far into the pond. He has grown several inches, it seems, since last summer, and his jaw seems stronger. Something has changed about his eyes.

He started talking about his father, how, when Willie was much younger, they would walk the banks of the Oconee River and they would fish and his Daddy would tell him stories about his Daddy, who died in a car wreck years ago. Willie did not smile as he remembered. His face was immobile, like that of a fifteenth-century saint. He said that once he had accidentally stepped into the edge of the river while they walked and got his boots wet and his father silently slid the belt from his pants and beat Willie terribly.

Then, when they got home, Willie's mother had found out about it and sneaked up behind his father and hit him in the back with a hammer.

"God, you've got to be kidding," I shuddered.

"They didn't really hate one another all that much," he said, reeling in a small bream. "They was just wont to act it sometimes."

February 17

Willie brought home his report card today. He failed math and history and made a C in geography and a D in English. I was beside myself with anger and self-pity.

"I ask you every night if you need help with your homework," I said.

"I don't need help. I don't really care none about books," he said without malice.

"You're going to fail this year," I said.

"I know," he said. Matter-of-factly.

"Don't you have any pride?"

"I wanna get a job. I ain't much for school, never was."

I sank heavily into a chair. I cannot bear the thought of my child being so bad in schoolwork, so indifferent to it. I was just blind and senile when I was teaching him here. We were both only using the other, he to hide and me to convince myself that I could still ply my trade.

I can't change him. I can't change.

February 18

It is nearly midnight, and the last coals from the fire are muted, glowing dimly in the fireplace. My coffee is getting cold. Willie is asleep under the electric blanket. I pull my robe tighter around me.

Africa is asleep at my feet, twitching and gnashing his teeth against some dream of rabbits flapping big-footed through the woods.

All these years gone. I never thought I would live so long. How was it my first day at Mt. Russell? I remember it all. I remember the way Sara's eyes looked when we walked down the row of dogwoods on her father's farm that night. He was so proud of those trees. I remember the way her hands felt when I clasped them to mine and asked her to marry me.

And I remember still further again my mother hanging out the wash in the bright spring sunshine, the clothes flapping in the wind, and me walking happily among the yard chickens, heading for the field and ruts where I pretended to be a Confederate soldier, daring and courageous perhaps at the Battle of Shiloh. I would rush between the lines and grab my friend from the grave's edge and dash back safely to our trenches with him to cheers from both sides of the lines.

But the only horse I slapped was my leg and the only glory I won was in my dreams. And yet I think that glory is best, the kind that comes without the burden of fame, glory in having persevered and done your best. All my life, I have been a character of marginal fame, having written books which few read and having taught thousands of students, most of whom would scarcely remember my name. And yet, on nights like this, when I settle into my dreamless memories, I pretend that to someone I made a difference, that among the icons of those various lives, I somehow live, not as the hero of Shiloh, but as a man of honesty who lived long, worked hard, and, in some measure, gained his rewards.

February 19

Bright sun streamed through the curtains this morning, almost like the early ghost of spring. Willie ate silently and slipped off to school. I will not call Callie today.

I feel like Theseus, as if I could grasp the thread of nature and my history and begin following it again, arm crooked with steel against every darkness.

I went down to Shadow Pond about noon and saw the beavers moving lordly in the water, no splashing. Trees have been gnawed down recently and the limbs clipped by those great yellowed fangs, dragged back to the lodges. I can almost imagine smoke coming from Indians' winter homes, thin filaments like feathers above a circle of hides on the prairie.

February 20

Callie came out today and we had a light lunch together. There is a strained silence sometimes between us and when we look at each other, some edge of guilt flares in our glance. Perhaps there is more fear than guilt.

"You been thinking about the Keys?" I asked.

"Sounds sort of nice," she said.

"Just sort of nice?"

"Well, intriguing." Flatly, strained.

"I think so."

Willie came home later and built a fire. When he pulled out a pack of Winstons and lit one, I said nothing because I was afraid he would become angry and leave me.

The way he looked at me said that I was weak, that I could not direct his life, and that I had no more right to be concerned than a kindly old neighbor.

February 21

I drove to Atlanta today with Charles, where he had some business to transact. I am struck with his great dignity. When we were children, he always carried himself well, and age has transformed posture into grace.

He talked about his grandchildren, telling me of his pride in young Charles, his namesake, who is in medical school in Augusta. For the first time in years, I talked about Jim.

"You never really get over something like that," I said.

"I wouldn't think so," he said, shaking his great head slowly from side to side.

"You don't know what to do with all the toys and things. It just leaves you feeling like you awakened from some dream of faith and purity to find only skepticism and sorrow spreading all over the world.

"It still hurts?"

"Not all the time. Sometimes. Some nights. Sometimes, things make me remember. Guess what it might have been like. But I lost all that years ago and I can't get it back."

February 22

While I was shaving to go to church this morning with Callie, Willie came into the bathroom and sat on the edge of the tub. He inhaled a cigarette and watched me in the mirror.

"Well?" I said.

"Nothing," he said.

He kept watching me, an unnerving thing to do to a man as he shaves.

"You want something?" I asked. He threw the cigarette into the john and it landed with a hiss.

"Nope."

"Just want to watch me shave?"

"I thought you might want some comp'ny."

"You want to go to church?"

"Nope."

240

"Well, that's up to you. I'm not forcing you."

"Okay."

He finally got up, put his hands in his pockets and went whistling out of the bathroom, leaving me to wonder what in the hell that was all about.

February 23

This journal has been a total failure. I'm not able to write what each day is like, only an incident or an anecdote. This is not so much a day book as a record of passing fancies and words my friends scatter on the wind.

Callie called today and said she was worried about her sister in Phoenix because her husband had had a severe heart attack and needed nursing all the time.

"I wish I didn't worry so much about her," she said.

I got the feeling she was trying to tell me something else, something far more important.

February 24

Willie didn't come home last night and I stayed awake all night waiting for him, drinking black coffee, clock-watching. I am unfit to be his guardian, but I fear his leaving more than I fear my failures with him.

But goddamnit! Damn this life all to hell! Why must there be so much agony mixed up with love? Why is there no true solace for an old man? Goddamnit! I started out to love nature and wound up more involved with people than I ever was in academic robes.

I called the school to tell them Willie was sick and they said he was there at school like always and I said what I meant to say was that he was feeling sick and might have to come home.

Liar! Son of a bitch!

February 25

I don't give a damn about anything.

February 26

Callie met me in town today at the Country Pine and she told me what I was afraid she would.

"Andrew, I've got to go to Phoenix for a while," she said. "I don't know how long. Maybe a couple of weeks. Carolyn needs some help and no one else is there."

"I see," I said. "You're good to go."

"You know what it means."

"Putting off the wedding."

"God, Andrew, I'm sorry," she said. "I'm so sorry. But only for a while. I was thinking it would be nicer in April or May, anyway, when it gets warm."

"Sure it would." I tried to smile.

When I got home this afternoon, I took a long walk in the woods, and drew some comfort. It was very cold, but the air was fresh and dry, and the sound of my footsteps on the leaves reminded me that I am still green, still alive, breathing.

There was a stillness in the woods that whispered to me the stories of dried ferns and tracks of mink and terrapin and Cooper's hawk. I kept inhaling as deeply as I could.

There is a reason for all this. No man can see life whole or understand this season. That is the dilemma of late love.

February 27

I drove Callie to the airport in Atlanta today and along the way, we were both surprisingly cheerful and talkative. She looked lovely, her eyes sparkling with excitement over the trip, not at all fearful of nursing her brother-in-law. She did, after all, nurse her late husband for months before his death.

When we finally parted, she to her plane and I back to the car, we kissed and I held her close to me.

"I'll miss you," she said.

"I love you, Callie," I answered. She patted me on the back like you do a spaniel.

"Well, keep yourself busy," she responded. I felt like a fool. I tried not to show it. Driving home, I tried not to think about her. I noticed how the pines and cedars stood out in a sea of forest brown. I noticed the crossing vapor trails of jets miles in the sky.

But it was no good. I brooded silently the last thirty miles. I feel I have begun to shed something like a skin.

February 28

Below me in the forest, there is life. More than tracks. Today was suddenly warm and I walked west, away from the pond for about half a mile and sat under a tulip tree and began to scrape the earth back from where it had been lightly frozen on top. I found a small knot of worms, a beetle of sorts that looked like a trilobite and a long caterpillar that waved its cilia at me in greeting, then burrowed deeper, out of the thin sunlight.

There is no trick to hiding. Animals are adapted both to escape and take camouflage among the trees and deep grasses. A brown thrasher can fade into the crisp, autumnal browns. The female cardinal, which bears the eggs that keeps the race alive, is less colorful than her mate and therefore less visible to predators, a protection when nest sitting.

Perhaps there is also grace in the way earthworms knot and twist for warmth (?) under the crystals of a frozen layer of dirt. Are there shades of darkness under the surface of the forest? What have they thought of my intrusion?

I held the worms in my hand and watched them turn. Was it against my terrible size, or against the sun that lay among the winter branches? Was it unkind to show them that there is also sun when it is not their season?

I thought on my way back how all this might apply to me,

but before the silly analogies could rise with my steps, I dismissed as contrived any such suspicion.

Spring is not far from awakening everything. I will listen this spring to every pulse I can find. But not of men. If it doesn't have greenery, feathers, fins or fur, I will not linger.

I do not know if there is a God or if there is goodness or evil in the earth. I have lost too much. I will praise what I can embrace.

March 1

Cold and rainy. I took Willie with me to Athens to help find some books for a monograph on Lieutenant William Fetterman, who led his men to death at Fort Phil Kearny. Willie looked at me suspiciously, but without malice or sympathy, a truly amazing combination.

I told him about Lieutenant Fetterman, and how he disobeyed his orders and led eighty men to their deaths at the hands of the Indians. He listened soberly, nodding sometimes, but listening withal.

I told him what Colonel Carrington said: "In the grave I bury disobedience." Willie nodded.

Deep in the corridors of the library, I reveled in the musty stacks, and found several references I had heretofore missed or forgotten. I had Willie copy several pages that were unimportant and when I checked his handwriting I discovered it was rather poor but legible. He did not complain.

I have not asked him why he was out all night earlier in the week. I think that perhaps he may respect me if I show our situation the mutual distrust it deserves. He shows no eagerness to confess.

When we got home late in the afternoon, the phone rang and it was Callie, who told me she had a good flight and the weather was nice out West.

March 2

I went to church at the Bethel Baptist Church today, and something terrible happened before I left. I wanted to ask Willie to come with me. But I must have been distracted. Maybe I am getting senile.

"Want to come with me, Jim?" I asked.

"Why'd you call me that?" he asked.

"Call you what?"

"You called me Jim. Why'd you call me that?"

"Good God, I did, didn't I."

"Why'd you call me that?"

"Just a slip of the tongue," I mumbled, horrified. I fell into a chair.

"Naw, I ain't going there."

In church, I tried to listen to what the preacher was saying, but I kept thinking of a roomful of unused toys, a rocking horse that was put in the back of a car and hauled away to a needy family nearby.

I kept seeing that rocking horse, with its blue and red ribbons blowing as I drove down the dirt road. I kept seeing those strong nostrils of that horse and those ribbons, like it was racing something, pursued by an army.

Do the dead grow older? Or do they grow younger into innocence? Should I pray for the latter?

March 3

The warm weather has exploded several pods of moss verbena *(Verbena tenuisecta)* in the woods back of my house. I looked them up in a book and read: "The fruit is an aggregate of four nutlets held tightly by the calyx."

What a lovely sentence. I can't picture a calyx holding a nutlet. I'd like to have tried that one out on Amos Crick.

Bill McAdam visited today after school. Willie did not show up until later, after Bill had left. Bill looks different since his father's death. His face is not one concerned with fishing or girlfriends. The world is too much with him.

"The worst part is you expect to see him every day," Bill said. "When you eat supper, you expect to see him."

"This world's not for sissies," I mumbled.

"No sir, that's a fact," he said.

We did not talk about that anymore, but we did talk about the baseball season to start in a few weeks, about the weather, about school. I felt sorry for Bill and told him to come out anytime he wanted to.

There is order in his sorrow. I understand that.

March 4

When I was a boy, I got lost one time. I was thinking about that today. I was going to walk from Uncle Roy's house back home down the road a mile, but I got the idea I could walk through the woods and get home quicker, even though it was getting dark before long.

I was only about eight or so, but I set off, figuring that if I kept walking on this straight line, I would have to get home. But darkness began to fall and I kept turning across fields I did not recognize and back into woods that left me disoriented.

I started running then, at first fast, but then a loose gallop and finally, a stumbling, gasping lope. Darkness overtook me and I started blindly going on until I fell into a tangle of blackberries, feeling the berries, ripe and heavy, smear on my cheeks as I fell.

I started crying. I was calling out. I thought I was going to die or be eaten by a wolf. Sometimes you could hear them growling around us in the night. They're all gone now.

Suddenly I heard my father's voice calling after me. I jumped up, fell, jumped up again, tearing long gashes in my arms and legs from the thorns. He found me and gathered me up into his strong arms.

I thought we would walk for miles and I was shivering against him when I realized we were only about two hundred yards from our house, just in the edge of the woods to the east. I had nearly made it on instinct.

I never forgot that. It didn't make me love persistence more. But it did keep me from exploring in the darkness.

March 5

I got a letter from Callie today, and its undertones were vague, even ominous.

"You know how a person stays all his life in one place and then sees a new land and is dazzled by it. I feel a permanent dazzle of the desert, Andrew. I could lie forever in the short grass when night comes and it is cool."

What could she mean by that? Will she not be coming back here? I think our plans have been mislaid among the ruins of illness and old age.

I'm scared. I look terrible in the mirror. I have been losing weight and my hair is coming out. I don't want to die yet. I'm scared of it.

March 8

No word from Callie on when she's coming back, and Willie seems so distant now I think I've lost him already. He looks at me differently, not with rage or love, but with a mixture of pity and indifference.

I didn't go to church today. What's the use? There's nothing there for me for faith or consolation. I am facing the abyss.

March 10

I had a terrible argument with Willie today. We were sitting on the front porch late in the afternoon and I told him to go do his homework. He said he didn't have any. I called him a liar, and he started yelling.

"I don't owe nobody nothing no more."

"Yeah, you're a goddamn big shot," I said.

"Least I ain't some old man." He spat out the last two words like a mouthful of wormy apple.

He left the house. It is nearly midnight as I write this and I don't know where he is.

March 15

What is wrong with me?

March 22

It's all over with Callie. She called me, said she was going to stay through the summer, sorry, etc. Told her I'm sorry, too, too bad about plans.

Just too damn bad.

Willie hanging around. I talked to his cousin in Greensboro. He said if I'm in a bad way come May, Willie can live there.

Told him thought it would happen.

April 2

It is hard for me to write, my hands shake so. Feel like something terrible is going to happen. I'm paying for something, but I don't know what.

Willie is helping me, maybe even a little tenderly. He is so tall and strong. Doesn't look like that little boy of a summer ago.

Poor Willie. My poor child.

April 9

My strength seems to be coming back. I called Callie today and we talked for a long time and she cried a lot. Her brother-in-law is well and back at work.

"I hate it out here," she said miserably.

"Why do you stay?"

"I'm scared of coming back."

"I've been awful sick anyway."

That upset her terribly and she said she would be flying back in a few days to take care of me.

"I'm not on death's door," I laughed.

"Don't tease me," she said.

"I just feel like I can't control anything anymore."

I do not know if this is the best thing. Why have these failures or our love grown so sacrificial?

April 10

I read today about the assassination of Lincoln and the conspiracy. It was rank injustice that Mary Surratt was hanged, that Dr. Samuel Mudd was sent to the Dry Tortugas.

Why is there such a rush to confirm our worst fears, a rush that sweeps into its vortex every kind and reasonable fact of survival?

In my rush to die, I have used the most selfish pity and callous joylessness. I have let the birds all turn into hovering crows, symbols of darkness and death. I have traded my love for a young boy for regret at the death of my Jim, blaming Willie perhaps that I have been for so long out of love with youth. When I taught, I was not in love with my students, but with my own erudition and the way I could trace my sensibilities on their hearts. Now they remain faithful, like Louis Percy, even if they fear me slightly for what I have given them.

I sat outside this warm afternoon with an afghan over my shoulders like a veteran of some forgotten war, home and brooding that the world holds nothing more terrible than those earlier wars, nor anything quite as beautiful.

April 11

This is a fine Saturday, and I am sitting on the banks of Shadow Pond with Willie and we are fishing. Callie called last night and said she would be back on Tuesday. I told her I was feeling a little stronger, which is the truth.

We are watching our bobbers float, and the air is so strong and clean I keep inhaling to enjoy it as much as I can. I feel slightly disembodied, almost ethereal, as if I were floating, too, drifting in the azure pond of the sky, outside of time and age.

Willie had done miserably in school and he has expressed few regrets. I told him about his cousin in Greensboro and he only nodded and shrugged.

But there is something different in his demeanor, a clear recognition of my predicament, perhaps, my inability to learn or teach, both of which make my life rich. But both are slowly returning.

Willie shows me how to bait a cricket, patient, graceful as wind. I lost my cricket to the weeds.

"I'll catch it," I say.

"Aw, let him go, Doc," Willie says. "Ain't nothing to 'em but legs and they don't cost nothing." He grabs another from the cage and hands it to me. This time I get it on and feel the power of death I have over it flow through me like blood.

The bream takes the line and I feel the power again, the mystery of this earth spread out before me under the growing shade of trees along Shadow Pond. I feel a quiet grandeur in the earth swelling like an organ note, and I rejoice that I am here and that I can breathe in the pure grace of the natural world.

April 12

At rest. Peace, almost.

Plato wrote: "When a man's pulse is healthy and temperate, and he goes to sleep cool and rational . . . having indulged his appetites neither too much nor too little, but just enough to lay them to sleep . . . he is then least likely to be the sport of fanciful and lawless visions."

My visions retract, expand, plunge forward, withdraw. They become clear as glacial water then opalescent as a cataract. Is this the common dilemma of mankind, to have vision circumscribed by sight?

I watched a pair of mourning doves for a long time today as they lingered in the boughs of the cedar next to the house, necks bobbing and extending, spearing movement with their turning eyes. But they did not move, content to watch and wait, snug in a warm breeze.

Today I have such an appetite, to watch from this small porch the life around me that does not turn or blink or scramble down the greening hill to the saving grace of water.

From the history of my life, I feel something deep and quenching, safe as love for a vulnerable child or someone laughing in your arms.

April 13

Tomorrow, Callie comes home. I tried on some shirts at a store in town, but the collars of my regular size are too big now and I had to go to a smaller size to fit. The sales clerk looked at me nervously and I merely shrugged and smiled.

When I got back to the car, I realized I had a large splotch of blood on my cheek where I'd cut myself shaving, and I felt like a fool for being so careless. I suppose that's one thing allowed the "aged," to be a slob without causing a scene.

When Willie got home from school, he went down to the pond with a pork and bean can full of raw calf's liver to fish for catfish. I watched him edge down the hill, and he moved stalk-straight, with a new kind of angularity.

Later, we skinned the six catfish he caught. I noticed Willie was bleeding on his left hand.

"What'd you do?" I asked.

"Sucker speared me," he sighed. "Getting him off the hook."

"You need something on it."

"Already put the slime on it," he grinned. "See?" He held his hand up into the fading sunlight and I could see a greasy wash across the blood where it dripped into his palm.

"I forgot," I nodded.

"It's okay," he said.

We ate the fish with buttered bread and applesauce and corn on the cob and nothing in my life ever tasted better.

April 14

I got to the airport and had a whiskey to calm my nerves waiting for Callie. When she finally came through the terminal, nearly lost in the crowd, I stood and looked at her and she caught my eyes and we both stopped and looked at each other for a moment. Then she came into my arms and we both looked into each other's eyes. I felt tears come up from somewhere.

"I feel like Odysseus come home," I said.

"But I'm the roamer," she said.

She told me I looked fine, but I could see in her eyes that she was concerned. I tried to project the peace I felt and she found my fingers and we held hands back to the car.

When we drove into town, she started crying.

"How could I leave all this," she said.

"You had to."

"Not as much as I had to come back."

Then I acted like some damned sentimental fool and I pulled into the road that winds through the cemetery where we used to walk and I cried, too.

The trees are coming back to life just now, and the new shadows covered the car as we moved slowly among the stones and our gentle words of regret and love.

April 15

We have agreed not to meet for a few days. I am overcome with sentiment and am aware that this is all surface, like the patina on the swampy edge of the pond. I scarcely know what I feel for Callie anymore. What drew her home was not me or my sickness, though I do not demean those motives, but instead the land, her home, and the mossy graves of her history.

Strangely, I got a letter from Hannah today. I haven't thought of her in months. She said she was just wondering how I was and so I wrote her back, old man to young woman, not fatherly at all, and without the transparent lack of wisdom I feel. I gave some advice. It's hard to stop being a teacher.

Bill McAdam stopped in this afternoon. He has been accepted as a student for the fall term at Mt. Russell! I told him I thought it was wonderful and that I regretted not being there to teach him history.

"Me, too," he mumbled shyly.

April 16

I have been keeping this journal nearly a year and perhaps it is time to rest, to latch it up and forget it. But not yet. I should put down what I have learned this year. I have forfeited my lifelong role as a teacher and tried to listen and learn, to sort out some fragment of truth among the ruins of this life.

I talked with Willie for a long time today. He seems brighter, more cheerful, but still out of love with any sort of academic life. He has already been told he will fail for the school year, though that was certain because of the days he missed at the first of the school year. But he could have survived with summer work. Not now. He shrugs.

"I just ain't that much of a student," he says.

But what should be learned and how should we learn it? Is it more honest to learn of the movements of battles and kings and countries or the movement of a catfish under a sunken log?

"You got me, Doc," Willie says.

Each man or woman is the child of history, the history of a life, whether in the order of words or the motion of the wind. How grand and foolish I sound!

It is nearly midnight, nearly a new day. I read from the book of Ecclesiastes:

> A good name is better than a good ointment, and the day of one's death is better than the day of one's birth. It is better to go to a house of mourning than to go to a house of feasting, because that is the end of every man, and the living takes it to heart. Sorrow is better than laughter, for when a face is sad, a heart may be happy. The mind of the wise is in the house of mourning, while the mind of fools is in the house of pleasure. It is better to listen to the rebuke of a wise man than for one to listen to the song of fools. . . . The end of a matter is better than its beginning.

April 17

Callie drove out today and we took a walk along the edge of the pond in the lovely, crisp spring air.

"Sometimes, a beaver will bubble up silently and swim toward me in the water," I said.

"What do they do when they see you?" she asked. I thought.

"Well, nothing much," I admitted. "They might flip and slap their tails in the water or they might just sink out of sight."

"Then what?"

"Oh, I always know they're around. They keep dams built, I see the young ones. Sometimes, I find their bones in the woods."

Later, after she had left, I took Daddy's spade and dug up a small lot in front of the house for some spring flowers. It will be nice to have some color among the green.

April 18

History no longer seems to interest me. I can only think of my friends and the small world around me here at Shadow Pond.

Willie and I drove to Greensboro today to talk to his cousin. Through the countryside, we talked little, only watching the road lazily unwind with us. We pulled up into his cousin's yard, a small patch of greenery at the edge of town. His cousin Brian Calvin's garden has already been turned and the fresh red earth nearly sparkled in the blue air. Brian's wife, Betsey, met us and took us in for tall glasses of iced tea.

They could not believe how much Willie had grown. We talked for a long time about insignificant things, avoiding what we had come to discuss. I told Willie to go outside and he slid away silently.

"I'm just getting too old to handle him," I said.

"You've done good by this family," Brian said.

"Sure have," Betsey said.

"But I can't have Willie with me anymore," I said. "I love him like a son, though." The words choked in my throat.

On the way home, everything having been settled, I could not look at Willie and he could not look at me. My hands kept shaking on the steering wheel, and I felt helpless and sad and wished I had died before I made these arrangements. Willie will leave me and move in with Brian and Betsey and their three kids at the end of May, if the court approves, and it has little choice. Willie will grow up and make his way without me, perhaps turning into a fine man, a strong one.

When we got home, Willie went fishing and I sat in the afternoon shadows of my house and listened to the song of a mockingbird.

April 19

There is no mystery in nature. I seek no hidden clues to the world in my walks. I only hope that somewhere among the lilies and lilacs and crawling vines I will learn to come to terms with my passion and my wonder for things that grow and prosper in their various seasons.

April 20

The dense fog covers the pond. I cannot see the water. But I hear the splash of *Castor* and know it is there. The fog hovers like icing over the earth. I huddle on my porch in a flannel shirt and peer into the whiteness.

This is the fog of the Battle of the Washita. Custer was a killer and a coward for that. But then it was bitterly cold and even the ponies made no sound before the light came.

Now, it is warm and still. The sun is there somewhere and I rejoice for its warmth. But its light fails now. There is only a wash across the earth, like memory or the first haze of desire.

April 21

Callie and I took a drive in the country today. I slumped in the seat like a very old man and my hands kept shaking. She has changed the way she looks at me.

How many years have passed since we first met?

"More than fifty years," she smiled. I nodded.

"We're fossils, Callie," I said.

"Speak for yourself." Laughter again. I am glad she is not given to being solicitous about my health. She will live for many more years. I just know it.

April 22

We talked.

"Why did you join the church when you did?"

"I just felt like it," Willie said.

"Why?"

"I felt sorta scared."

"Of what?"

"Something out there."

"What?"

"I don't rightly know."

I can't write anymore.

April 23

My left leg has gone numb on me. I think it's serious this time. I don't know what else to think.

I've got to get some bread today. And milk.

April 24

Can't concentrate. I hear secrets in my head.

April 25

I feel no stronger but my hand is steady and my head is clear. I can't get warm so I got Willie to build me a fire in the fireplace before he left. I think he's gone to visit Carleen. Haven't heard from her in some time.

I sit here by the fire and wait.

April 26

I got up the strength to take a walk today. The world was green and moving in the breeze. As I walked, I tried to sing some old hymns like "How Firm a Foundation" and "Faith of Our Fathers," but my voice is a hoarse croak. I walk so slowly it takes me forever to get around.

I found a nest of robins' eggs, rich and blue. I stood tiptoe and looked at them for a long time but I did not touch them. I do not understand why the inside of the nests is so smooth or why the eggs are so brightly blue.

I do not understand that at all. Perhaps it is what God intended. Or maybe it is what the robins intended. I do not know.

April 28

Exhausted from my walk, I didn't write yesterday. I keep going to sleep for a long time. My right leg is starting to get numb on me.

I should call a doctor.

April 29

I'll stay here. I'll crawl down by the pond while Willie is at school with his lessons, just curl up.

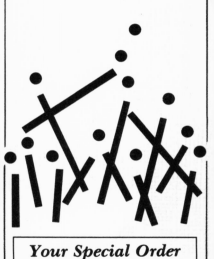

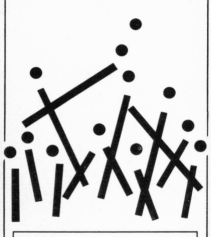

April 30

A year since I started this damn thing. No more writing. I can't get out of bed at the moment. Callie is here and she looks worried.

The day is soft and still, and the stillness is in me.

And even then, Callie is worried.

But why, love?

In my heart is the song of fools. But I will sleep with the dust of kings.

About the Author

Philip Lee Williams lives with his wife and son in Athens, Georgia. He is the editor of the Athens *Observer*.